JASON STEED

BY ROYAL DECREE

MARK A. COOPER

DEDICATION

To Sandra, you are the reason why I look
forward to waking up everyday.

www.markacooper.com

Library of Congress Catalogue-in-Publication data is on file with the author.

CHAPTER ONE

"How much longer are you gonna keep this up?" Shamus shouted.

"Keep what up?" Maude asked, slamming down his dinner so hard on the table most of the peas spilled off the plate and ran across the vinyl tablecloth.

Bradan smiled as he watched the peas run across the table. He climbed from the chair and left his brother and sister-in-law to argue. The O'Neill's told everyone Bradan O'Neill was still-born thirty-eight years earlier. The hospital staff fought to save him and eventually had brought him back to life. His brain was damaged, and as a result, he had a mental age of a four-year-old. He would be held in a mental asylum if it wasn't for his younger brother Shamus taking him in. Shamus's wife Maude helped look after him.

The family lived in a small three-bedroom local authority home on McDonald Street, in the Lower Falls area of Belfast,

Northern Ireland. Maude worked at the local grocers. She stood just under five foot tall with shoulder length red hair. She married Shamus, her school sweet heart, ten years earlier. The couple argued frequently. They had been unable to conceive a child, and after constant arguing or nagging as Shamus called it, he finally agreed with Maude that they would adopt a child.

However, having a retarded thirty-eight year old man in the home became an obstacle to adopting an infant. Social services were concerned that Bradan was clumsy and being in the home was not a safe environment for a tiny baby.

"Okay, I'll come to the meeting tomorrow but it seems like a waste of time to me. You'll only get upset when they turn us down again." Shamus affectionately placed his hand on the back on Maude's hand. She smiled back at him before settling down and started eating her dinner. Maude loved Shamus; it took just a smile and she would do as he asked. Shamus was a tall, thin man, usually unshaven with a cigarette hanging from the corner of his mouth.

But his broad smile and large brown eyes melted Maude's heart. She had adored him since they were at school together.

*

Shamus and Maude were shown into a meeting room and asked to wait for caseworker Jerry Duffy. Plastic toys spilled out of a trunk in the center of the room. The walls were painted with rainbows, fluffy white clouds, and characters, mostly dwarfs from the Disney movie Snow White. Maude clutched her purse tight, her curly red hair bouncing off her shoulders as she looked around the room, finding it hard to contain her excitement.

"Ah Shamus and Maude top of the morning to ya." Jerry Duffy smiled. The little Irish man paced into the room and shook the couple's hands. He stood no taller than five foot and had a gap where his two front teeth should have been. It gave him a lisp as he spoke.

"Do you have any news on our application for the adoption yet?" Maude asked.

"Maude." Jerry paused. "I can call you Maude and Shamus I hope? If 'twas up to me, I'd be giving you a baby today, but other workers on your case are concerned about Bradan, after he hurt that wee boy a few years ago."

"That *wee boy,* as you put it, was fourteen and stealing Bradan's drawings. He deserved to get his arse kicked," Shamus argued. "Bradan doesn't have much. His drawings may seem like nothing to others but they are everything to him."

"Shamus, I'm on ya side, but others think he's off his nut and worried if you had a baby or a little snapper in the home who touched his drawings… Well you can see their point?" Jerry said.

Shamus looked at Maude. "I told ya this would be a waste of time." Maude's eyes welled up. She and Shamus had been hoping to have a baby, but after ten years of marriage, nothing had happened. She longed to have a child of her own. It made matters worse sitting on the sidelines and watching as her friends give birth to multiple children.

Jerry opened a file and smiled. "I do

have something that might cheer you up. It's not a baby, but it's a child who needs a family. To start with, we just need to find him a foster family, but if you like him and he likes you, then maybe we can consider something more permanent."

"Him?" Maude said excitedly. "How old is he?"

Jerry looked back at the file. "He's twelve. He just arrived in our care. I don't know much about him. He was born in Belfast and has been living with an adopted family in England. Apparently, the adopted parent died a few years ago and he has been bounced around a few foster families. Social services in England think it may be easier for him back in Belfast."

"Twelve, that's nice. I have a niece that age. Can we meet him?" Maude asked. She looked at Shamus for approval. He nodded and held her hand.

"Well, he'll be here tomorrow. I can bring him to your home. These older children can be a challenge. They sometimes have issues and need just as much love and care as a wee baby."

CHAPTER TWO

Twelve-year-olds Jason Steed and Scott Turner travelled by Royal Air-Force transport plane to Shackleton Army barracks in Northern Ireland. They had spent the last three days reading and going over Jason's cover story for his undercover mission.

They were very close friends but couldn't be mistaken as brothers. Scott was thin, his skin white as if it had never seen the sun. His short hair brown matched his large brown eyes. Jason was slim and walked with confidence, his hair blond, short at the back and side and long in the front. His bangs covered his blue eyes.

As expected, Scott being extremely intelligent had picked it up faster. He bombarded Jason with question after question until Jason had the information planted deep in his memory. The army barracks were to be Scott's home for the next few weeks while Jason was undercover. Should Scotland Yard Undercover Intelligence (SYUI) need to get information from Jason, Scott would be used as his contact.

No one would suspect anything suspicious of two twelve-year-old boys talking together. The boys were taken into a room by George Young, head of SYUI, who had travelled on ahead. He met the boys in the corridor.

"Nice flight, boys?" George asked.

"Are you kidding? It was a military plane. It was noisy, cold, and stunk of oil." Scott said. Jason looked on, saying nothing. He knew it was only a matter of time before he was whisked away and undercover. He hated telling lies to people. He had gone undercover with a family once before, and he had struggled emotionally with the situation.

George took the boys into an office with a metal brief case in the center of the table.

"This is for you, Jason. It will help you with this mission," George said and gently opened the case. Both boys peered inside. Jason's smirk quickly changed to a frown. Scott's eyes beamed.

"Is this a joke? If it is, it's not very funny." Jason scowled.

"That is way cool," Scott said. He picked up the brown grubby teddy bear from the case and started to examine it. Jason looked at his friend in wonder.

"Scott I know you better than that. Even *you* still don't have a teddy," Jason said.

"You are one smart cookie Scott." George smiled. "How could you tell it's not just a cuddly toy?"

"It's not?" Jason asked, looking even more mystified.

"Well George, you're hardly likely to be giving Jason a cuddly toy. He's about to go undercover in the home of an IRA bomber. What's in it? A gun? A bomb? A laser? Do the eyes shoot bullets?" Scott paused, examining the Teddy bear more. "Oh, he's only got one eye."

"What are you two talking about?" Jason asked.

George took the teddy bear from Scott. "Jason on this mission you get gizmos," George said.

"Gizmos?"

"You know Jason, just like James Bond had tear gas disguised as talcum powder or that cigarette that could shoot out a bullet or a pen that could do the same and lasers," Scott said.

"But how did you know that the teddy was

a gizmo?" Jason asked his friend.

"Why else would it be in a metal case and opened for you by the head of SYUI?"

Jason shrugged his shoulders. "What does it do?"

George explained. "Pull his button eye and twist it to the right and it starts recording. Both ears have powerful microphones built in. To replay it back, you have to turn the eye back to the left and push it in again. Then, push the nose twice. A miniature speaker is fitted in his mouth. It's not going to be loud but loud enough for you to hear if you hold its mouth to your ear." He demonstrated.

"So if I want to listen to what I recorded I have to cuddle it and have it almost kissing my ear?" Jason smiled.

"Yes, look after Charlie well. Now, we have to move. We have work to do," George said passing the teddy bear to Jason.

"Charlie?"

"Charlie Ted. Call him that. The story is you have had him for as long as you remember and you keep him as a comforter."

"But I'm twelve," Jason whined.

"You're also an orphan with no family, so anything like Charlie gives an orphan some familiarity and something to hug. You never know, you might get to like him," George said.

"Can I take Jason's picture holding his teddy bear?" Scott said.

"Not if you want to live," Jason snapped, glaring at his friend.

George took them into another room where a man was waiting at a desk.

"Jason, this is Paddy Murphy. He is going to take you to meet your real social worker, a gentleman called Jerry Duffy," George said.

Jason looked up at the man and shook his hand, followed by Scott who was grinning.

"Paddy Murphy? That's a bit over the top don't you think. Surely you could have come up with a better name than that?" Scott laughed. The man pulled back his hand from Scott and glared at him.

"That's my name, it is," Paddy Murphy said in a broad Irish accent.

"Oh. Sorry, it just seemed a bit obvious," Scott said.

"Well, you're in bloody Ireland now so get used to it," Paddy said. He turned and looked at Jason who had a large smirk on his face. He seemed as if inspecting something for damage. "And as for you Jason, get those posh clothes off. You've come from a foster home; you can't go in wearing that. And your shoes." He passed Scott a bag of clothing. "Help your friend get ready; we need to move. Jerry Duffy will be waiting, he will. And why is your hair so long? I can't see your eyes."

"That's Jason. He always has long hair in the front," Scott said as he opened the carrier bag and pulled out the clothing and shoes they had chosen.

"Can he not speak for himself?" Paddy asked, looking at Jason.

"I can keep my jeans. Jeans are just jeans," Jason said.

Paddy looked down at him, his face inches away from Jason.

"You're wearing bloody new Wranglers and Nike trainers. Get them off," Paddy said, prodding Jason with a pair of jeans from the bag.

11

"These jeans are what foster children wear, cheap ones from the market."

Jason took a deep breath and undressed to his underwear and picked up the jeans provided for him. They were used, torn and frayed at the bottoms He pulled them up, hoping they would not fit. Scott picked up a pair of grayish baggy underpants and waved them at Jason with a grin across his face.

"Jase, you gotta put these on too," Scott said.

"No one is going to get close enough to see what undies I wear. I'm keeping mine on," Jason said. No one argued. He pulled on a loose fitting vest and topped it off with a blue hand knitted jersey. His new Nike trainers were replaced with a pair of used and scuffed school shoes. "At least they fit." He sighed and felt the loose material hanging from his backside. "Although these are hanging off me."

"Of course they fit you. We have planned everything to fine detail. Now say your goodbyes to Scott and let's go," Paddy ordered.

Scott looked at his friend and smiled. "I like the look. You would fit in with a bunch of rotters from a housing estate."

"I think that's the whole idea. I wish I was staying at the base. It looks much more fun than where I have to go," Jason said. He forced a smile. He went to shake Scott's hand goodbye, then thought about a hug and then thought better of it. That was girly, so he ended up with a pat on his friends shoulder. Scott felt just as awkward and patted Jason's arm.

George came back into the room and looked at Jason. "Okay son, do us proud again. We need as much information on this lot as you can get. Every little detail could save a life or more. If we can find out who supplies the IRA with weapons and explosives, you are saving the lives of many plus saving the terrible injuries that they inflict. And if you can get the name of the head guy of the IRA, that would be ideal but probably impossible. And most important, more important than anything else, you must do one thing for me," George said.

"What's that?" Jason asked, thinking he had missed something.

"Jason, please..." George paused and placed his hand on Jason's shoulder. "Please look after yourself. Don't take any risks. This is a brutal war. We are not here to take sides. You can't take on the IRA. Just get the information and get out."

Jason couldn't swear on it but was sure he noticed George's eyes welled up slightly. "I will, George. I'm just a poor little orphan going to live with a family, who just happened to blow up my grandparents," Jason said.

"We suspect Shamus was responsible, Jason. That's all, but we have enough to know he is a high-ranking IRA officer. We need more than that. Taking him off the streets won't stop the bombs going off. We need the suppliers and the man at the top issuing the orders," George said.

Paddy looked at his watch. "Mr. Young, we have to get going. Come along, Jason, it's time to go to work." Paddy packed the additional sets of clothing into a case and placed Charlie Teddy on top before closing it.

Jason followed Paddy outside to a yellow Ford Cortina. They never spoke to each other as they drove out of the barracks towards the center of Belfast. Jason watched the scenery flash by. He thought Northern Ireland looked like parts of Britain, mostly the run down parts. Slogans and memorials such as 'Brits out' and 'Sinn Fein Rules' decorated homes, many covered the whole house from the base to the roof.

Another building was painted red with the Ulster Freedom Fighters slogan and the image of a hooded man with a gun. Among the political slogans was a house painted with a picture of George Best, an Irish soccer star. When a sign read 'Free Derry' the area seemed more run-down, with more derelict homes. Many with windows boarded up.

Eventually, they stopped at Belfast Council Social Welfare offices. Paddy parked the car. He caught the curb with one wheel. He tried again, this time the back wheel was on the curb. He gave up and turned the engine off. Jason made a mental note not to trust Paddy's driving.

"Okay we're here," Paddy said. Jason never spoke. He was tentative, a mixture of excitement nervousness, dreading who he would be meeting, where he would be eating and sleeping. The jersey had already started to make him itch around his neck.

Jason followed Paddy into the offices. They were met by Jerry Duffy.

"Hello, young man. You must be Jason Norris. Welcome back to Ireland." Jerry smiled. Jason had chosen the undercover name Norris again, rather than Steed, after his idol, the world karate champion, Chuck Norris.

"Hi," Jason quietly replied.

"Have all the barber shops in England

gone on strike?" Jerry asked.

Jason looked puzzled. He was unsure of what he had said. The Irish accent was taking a while to adjust to. "What, who's on strike?" Jason asked.

"Why is your hair so long, boy?" Jerry asked and smiled, rocking back and fourth on his heels.

"I don't know it just keeps growing. Maybe I should stop eating," Jason replied in a contemptuous tone.

Jerry raised his eyebrows at Paddy. "Maybe it was a long journey and he's tired. Okay Paddy, I'll take it from here. It was nice meeting you. I'll take Jason to meet the O'Neill family."

*

Jerry stopped his car outside the O'Neill's home on McDonald Street. Jason sluggishly climbed out the car and looked up and down the street. It was empty, apart from a few old parked cars. There was no sign of activity on this street, but he knew from the twitch of a curtain or two from neighboring homes that someone had noticed his arrival.

McDonald Street was a row of thirty or so

identical terraced stone built homes. Each one had a different color front door. The O'Neill's home had a red front door; they did not own a car.

Maude O'Neill opened the front door and beamed when she saw Jason looking up at her. He parted the blond fringe of hair that hung over his eyes and smiled back at her.

"Maude, this is Jason Norris. Jason, this is Mrs. O'Neill," Jerry said.

"Jason, what a nice name. You'll be needing your hair cut soon." Maude smiled.

"Hello," Jason said, deliberately ignoring the hair cut remark.

She showed Jason into the home. He took in his surroundings. The home was small and clean but had a strong smell of cigarettes. A haze of smoke hung on the ceiling. It was previously white but was now nicotine stained yellow. He was shown into the front room. A television boomed with coverage of a soccer match. Shamus and Bradan O'Neill were sat together on a brown couch. Jason waved the smoke away from his face. Both men starred at Jason and looked him up and down. Shamus stood and shook Jason's hand.

Jason watched the curious, impressive profile of Shamus for a time. Was this the man who killed his grandparents? A part of him felt like hurting him, but for now he had a mission to do. He would go along with it. Jason studied him. He looked older than his thirty-six years. His hair had prematurely turned grey. He wore a white shirt and black pants.

"Top of the morning to you Laddie." Shamus Smiled. "Welcome to our home. I'm Shamus O'Neill your new foster father and you are?"

"This is Jason, Jason Norris," Maude interrupted.

"Jason, we were watching the match. Ho you like soccer? Oh this is my brother Bradan," Shamus said. Jason looked at Bradan, he was an older version of Shamus, with watchful eyes. He said nothing, his eyes watching the television and then back to Jason's, trying not to make eye contact. Jason stepped forward. He had been briefed on the case by Jerry and was told Bradan had some mental health issues.

"Hello, Bradan, I'm Jason. Nice to meet you, sir," Jason said.

"He's English," Shamus snapped at Jerry, his eyes glaring at Jason as he climbed out of his seat. "Are you taking me for an Eejit?"

"Ee what?" Jason asked, looking at Shamus and back at Jerry.

Shamus laughed and calmed down. "I was talking to Jerry, not you Laddie."

"Shamus, he's Irish. He has been with English foster families, but according to his records he was born in Belfast. I'm sure once we get him into a local school he will drop that accent," Jerry said. "Jason, Eejit is Irish for Idiot."

"Oh." Jason laughed.

"Come on Jason, let me show you around the house. This is your home now," Maude said. Jason followed her into the kitchen. "Can I get you a drink? I have orange. We don't have any Coke. I'm making a fresh pot of tea, do you like that?"

"Yes, tea is great. Thanks, Mrs. O'Neill," Jason said. She filled the kettle and took Jason up stairs. She showed Jason the bathroom. It was small, no shower but a large cast iron bathtub, a sink with three toothbrushes scattered along the back, a trail of dried crusted toothpaste ran across the top of the sink. The toilet had a fluffy orange cover on the lid. "I will put out a towel for you later."

She stopped outside the bathroom door and waited for Jason on the landing. Slowly, she opened the first bedroom door. "This is Bradans room. Apart from now, you will have no need to enter it. Jason followed her in. It had a single bed under the window and pictures hanging on every wall. Jason found them hard to understand, some looked like horses and dogs with lines going through them, others plants or trees.

"Bradan has a few issues and can't think like we do. He loves his drawings; please do not ever touch them or come into his room. He's harmless enough but he likes his privacy," Maude said.

"I understand, Jerry told me. I won't bother him," Jason said.

"This is mine and Shamus's room." She pointed before opening the door at the end of the landing. "And this will be yours, it's wee but comfortable." Jason stepped into the small bedroom. It was the smallest bedroom he'd ever seen. The single bed fitted snug with no room at either end. It had a dresser against the wall and a small wooden chair under the window. There was just enough room to walk between the bed and dresser.

Jason peered out the window and turned back to Maude. "It's a nice room. Thank you for having me."

Maude placed his case on the bed and opened it. She smiled. "And who do we have here?" She took out Charlie Teddy.

Jason blushed and went into his act. "I don't need that old thing now I'm twelve. I've had it for years. Probably throw it away soon. I don't need it to get to sleep," Jason said.

"Then should I be giving him to the church for a charity sale?" Maude asked.

"Um no, I'll just put him on the bed He brings me luck," Jason said, trying to look embarrassed. She placed his clothing in the dresser and slid the case under his bed. Charlie was tucked in the bed with his head sticking out the top, his one button eye looking up at the ceiling.

The O'Neill's chose Shankill High School, mostly because the majority of the students were Catholic. It took students aged from eleven to sixteen and was a fifteen-minute walk from the home. Maude took Jason his first day to complete the enrollment paperwork. Jason wore black trousers, white shirt, and grey 'V' neck pullover. The school had no set uniform. They tried to encourage all religions, however protestant families preferred Downsview High School that was a half a mile away.

Jason received looks from most of the children in the corridor. He expected it; he was the new boy after all. He felt relaxed and was happy not to wear a tie or a school uniform. Jason had only been to all-boys schools. He wondered how it would differ from what he was used too.

A bell sounded and the corridors soon emptied. The children branched off into the class rooms, a couple of late stragglers ran in and where abruptly shouted at by the headmaster, Mr. Filan, for running.

"Maude O'Neill, this is a nice surprise, and who do we have here?" Mr. Filan asked. He paced towards them and shook Jason's hand.

"Kian Filan, it's good to see you, although I'm sure you're Mr. Filan here in the school. This is Jason, Jason Norris. I'm his foster mother and have come to enroll him," she said proudly. Mr. Filan looked back at Jason.

"Welcome to Shankill High, Jason. I'm sure you'll soon fit in and make plenty of friends.

Your hair is long at the front, can you see out?"

"Thank you sir. I can see just fine thanks," Jason said, brushing his blond bangs across his eyes.

"Well if you say so. Let's do some paperwork and get you in class."

Before she left, Maude looked at Jason and straightened his collar. "Bless you and keep out of trouble," she said and kissed him on the forehead.

If anyone had been looking, Jason would have blushed with shame. But as it was, the kiss and blessing lightened his heart as he walked away.

Jason cringed when he walked into the class. He could feel everyone's eyes watching him. He pulled his blond bangs across his face so it hung just below his eyes. Even at the age of twelve, it still acted as a barrier for him; it made him feel secure. His hair was always cut short on the back and side, but hung long on top over his eyes. He would argue it was his fashion statement, but if the truth was known, it was for times like this when his shy side took over and he wanted to hide in his comfort zone.

The first lesson was math, followed by

English. Jason found the lessons surprisingly easy. In the private School he had attended, he was below average in all subjects except languages. Here at Shankill he seemed to be above average in everything.

The bell rang for the end of morning period; it was morning break. Jason followed the other children. A few visited the bathrooms and the rest made their way to the playground. Jason stood alone, taking his surroundings. Some of the younger girls played a clapping hands game; it amused him. The older boys walked in groups, some younger boys ran after each. A game of soccer took part in the center. Jason couldn't make out who was against who. It seemed like they were all against each other and not in specific teams.

He was nudged in the shoulder. "Watch it blond mop," A boy said. Jason quickly turned. A boy his age he noticed in class faced him.

"Sorry I didn't see you," Jason said.

The boy stood back. Jason sized him up. He looked twelve, stocky with short dark hair with green eyes that looked too close together. "Are you English?" he asked excitedly.

Jason could see the eagerness in his question. He wasn't sure if he could pull off an

Irish accent but knew as soon as he answered it would be trouble. "No I was born in Belfast. I've been to school in England for a few years but I'm home now."

"You sound like an English toff. What are you doing 'ere?" the boy demanded.

"I live here now with foster parents," Jason said, slowly twisting himself at an angle to the boy and raising himself on his toes. He was expecting trouble although he knew he couldn't possibly use his martial arts skills on a schoolboy. But he was not about to get hurt either.

"I don't like the English." The boy moved forward and tried to grab Jason's collar. His attempt was blocked. Jason paused. He was told never to use his skills and knew he had to be careful in situations like this. A playground brawl could prove deadly to someone. The decision was made for him the boy swung a fist towards Jason's face.

Jason ducked and held his own fist back, not wanting to hurt the boy. The boy swung again and again. Each time, Jason blocked the blows.

"Scrap," someone shouted, then another. A crowd gathered; jeers and cheers followed. "Go on Haden, give it to him." Not getting anywhere with his fists, the boy they called Haden kicked out at Jason. Instinctively, Jason blocked it and swept Haden's other leg away, sending Haden onto the ground. Jason held himself back. He would normally pounce. Instead, he stood back.

Haden climbed to his feet. His face was bright red. Jason wasn't sure if it was anger or embarrassment. Haden lunged at Jason, but his move was predictable and slow. Jason twisted to one side and, using a judo technique, threw Haden into crowd of spectators. The failing attempt to hurt Jason lost Haden any supporters he had. They stepped back and let him fall to the ground.

Haden climbed to his feet again, his face bright red, sweating and gritted teeth. Again, he ran at Jason with fists flying. Jason blocked the first punch and caught Haden's arms and held it in an arm lock.

"When you let me go I'm going to kick your head in," Haden cursed. Jason held his arm firm. Haden screamed in pain. "Let us go, you blond haired wazzock."

Jason applied more pressure to Haden's arms and bent down towards Haden's face and spoke quietly in his ear. "Listen you little Dodo, you either calm down and leave me alone or I'll break your arm," Jason said before he applied more pressure and let him go, pushing Haden away.

Haden recovered and rubbed his arm. "You're lucky you caught me off guard with a bad arm, else I'd take ya easy," Haden shouted.

"Yeah Haden, looks like he's shaking in his boots. Just admit it, you got your head kicked in by the new boy." An older boy chirped in and laughed. Haden ignored the remark and stormed off, leaving Jason in the center of the crowd. Jason put his hands in his pockets and walked through the crowd. They moved away, giving him an exit.

"Hey what's your name?" another boy asked. He ran and caught up with Jason.

"Jason Norris." He turned and looked at the boy. He had red hair and more freckles than Jason had ever seen on one person. They covered his face, neck, and even his ears. He wore round wire glasses. He was thin and his clothing was much too large for him and hung off his small body. Jason assumed it was passed down from an older brother.

"I'm Gobnait O'Grady," he said.

Did he seriously say Gobnait? Jason said to himself.

"Hi, Um what did you say your name was again?" Jason asked.

"Gobnait O'Grady. Most just call me Gober." He paused and continued. "Well, my friends do anyway; the others call me Nerdnait here."

"Why *Nerdnait*?" Jason asked.

"'Cause I'm good at math, English and well most of it, and I read a lot of books."

How do I always attract the nerds? Jason asked himself.

"Can I call you Gober?" Jason smiled.

"Yes, what do they call you, just Jason?

"Normally, although today, Haden called me blond mop." Jason grinned.

"Well that's cause you got long blond hair." He examined Jason. "Well long in the front. You can't see your eyes. How come you never hit Haden, you had plenty of chances? Everyone would love to hit Haden McGinty. All the McGinty's think they're hard."

The bell sounded before Jason could answer. They walked back to class. Jason was

surprised that no teachers turned up to break up
the fight. It almost seemed acceptable practice

CHAPTER THREE

The next period was French. It was a subject he was top in at his previous school, St. Joseph's. Even Scott, with his extremely high IQ, couldn't match Jason when it came to foreign languages. Jason put it down to learning both English and Chinese as a child after being born and brought up in Hong Kong at the British Naval base. Since then, he had been able to pick up a foreign language quickly.

Jason waited for most of the children to take a seat before finding an empty space. The closest one was next to a girl he later found out was called Danni. She was a slim girl with pretty blue eyes, long brown shoulder length hair, and a dimple in her chin.

"Is anyone sitting here?" Jason asked.

"Not unless they're invisible," she tutted. "There's a space back there with Gober." She nodded with her head. Jason looked up. Gobnait was smiling at him, beckoning him back.

After finally sitting next to Gobnait, the teacher, a Mrs. Tetley, walked in. She was a large woman with a friendly face.

"Bonjouer," Mrs. Tetley announced.

The class greeted her with the same welcome. The lesson was painfully boring for Jason. He kept his French skills to himself. He wanted to keep under the radar. He had already been in the limelight too much for one day. Although he noticed Danni looking at him, when he looked back, she turned her head away as if she wasn't interested in him.

Final lesson of the day was math. Jason found it surprisingly amusing. Mr. Griggs, the math tutor, was a spry little old Irishman with long gray hair, wild green eyes, and frequent nervous twitches. His Irish drawl amused Jason so much he had to hold off from laughing.

Jason gave a sigh of relief when the final bell went off, signaling end of the school day. He was pleased to get out of school. A sense of freedom hit him when he got outside, then reality set in. He wasn't going home. He was going to the O'Neill family home.

He opened the front door, kicked off his shoes, and walked into the kitchen. He was surprised to see a group of six men sat around the table.

"Who the bloody hell is this?" one man with no teeth asked, getting up from his seat.

Bradan was sat with them. He frowned at

Jason and, as usual, said nothing. The room went silent, most of the men looked at Bradan as if he was going to say something. Jason found that weird, as Bradan never said hardly anything.

"I'm Jason. I live here. Who are you? Where's Maude and Shamus?"

"Relax guys this is Jason. He's Maude's, well *our,* foster son," Shamus said, strolling into the kitchen doing up his fly.

"He sounds English, Shamus," the toothless man said, although Jason thought he whistled the word Shamus.

"He does, but he's Irish blood in him just been in school over there for a few years. We'll soon get him speaking proper again. Won't we Jason? How was your first day at school?" Shamus said.

"Um, okay thanks. Can I get a drink please?"

"Sure, the guys just came around for a chat. They're leaving now. See you at the Red Bull tonight lads," Shamus said.

The group of men got up and slowly left. A few ruffled Jason's hair and smiled at him.

"Help yourself to a drink laddie. Maude got some orange squash or extra milk for ya. She's at the chip shop getting our dinner. She won't be long."

"Thanks," Jason said and poured himself a glass of milk.

"So everything go well at school Jason, make any friends?" Shamus asked suspiciously. Jason picked up on his tone and noticed Bradan watching and waiting for an answer.

"Yes sir, I made a new friend. Gobnait O'Grady."

"Ah that'll be Mick's youngest boy. Had eight kids Mick O'Grady did. One died in a car accident. But a good family I hear that. That Gobnait's a smart kid; you'll do good to stick with him." Shamus paused and tilted his head to one side, looking at Jason. "Anything else happen?"

Jason wiped his mouth and milk moustache with the back of his hand and placed the empty glass in the kitchen sink.

"Um, yeah I sort of got into a fight at break time. I never hit anyone I just bent his arm back." Jason struggled with the words. His own father would be furious if he got into a fight

33

because of the damage he could do. Shamus, however, didn't know of his skills.

"I have friends everywhere. We heard it was with one of the McGinty boys. Tough lot they are. Did you get hurt much? When I heard it was with one of them well, I thought you would be coming home black and blue. What with you being so…" he paused. "You know."

"No?" Jason asked. He felt annoyed by the tone Shamus used and not sure what he was insinuating.

"Well I'm guessing you've been living with a posh family. You have a slightly upper crust accent not all the time but now and again you drop out something and you still sleep with a teddy. I just assumed you were a…" He paused again, trying to get the correct words. "Well, you know, the gentle type of lad."

Jason paused in deep thought. He realized Shamus was smarter than he gave him credit for. *Of course I sound posh. My father's an officer in the Royal Navy, my girlfriend is a princess, and I go to one of England's top private schools. I speak properly but I guess it sounds posh to some*, he said to himself.

"Charlie Teddy is the only family I have, after going from home to home. It's nice to have one thing that's always the same. Haden McGinty tried to hit me, I dodged and caught his arm and bent it back. It was not a real fight. I'm sorry. I won't get in a fight again."

"No need to be sorry. Laddie. Boys are boys and boys fight; makes you a man. No problem here. I'm glad to hear it, although Maude wasn't happy to hear you were fighting on your first day of school. Me, Ha, I'm proud of you, fighting with a McGinty. Tough bunch they are. The Creggan Cleaners kneecapped fifteen-year-old Josh McGinty last month."

"Kneecapped, what's that mean?" Jason asked.

"They blow your bloody knee cap off with a shotgun, and the Eejit deserved it. For months he had been stealing cars, radios from cars, milk from peoples doorsteps, including the elderly, and the last straw came when he stole the purse of Mrs. O'Hara. A week earlier she laid her husband to rest," Shamus said.

"So this group *Creggan Cleaners* they shot his kneecaps? Why didn't the police just arrest him?" Jason paused. "And the group Creggan Cleaners? They can't go around shooting people."

"Creggan Cleaners is a group of local people, mostly from Creggan, Derry. Some members are police. They take care of trouble makers. Let that be a warning to ya laddie, never break the law if you want to keep your kneecaps. I heard the hospital had to amputate his leg. He was lucky not to die from loss of blood."

"Yeah I'll be sure to keep out of trouble," Jason said, he was shocked and was sure Shamus knew more than he was letting on about the group.

It wasn't long before Maude came home with the fish and chips. They all ate it at the table out of the newspaper. When dinner was done, Shamus left to meet his friends at the Red Bull pub. Bradan went up to his room. Maude and Jason watched television together.

As Jason lay in his bed that night staring at the ceiling, he reflected on the day. The school had been what he had expected, shy girls acting tough, the local bully throwing his weight around with the new kid, trying to establish pecking order. Something at the house wasn't sitting right with Jason, yet he couldn't quite put his finger on it.

He wasn't too surprised Shamus heard about the fight. After all Shamus is well known, if he is who George Young thinks he is then Shamus is just being careful. No it was something else, something was not right with the way the others had acted around Bradan. Maybe they felt sorry for him and tried to make him feel like one of the guys. Yes, Jason thought, it had to be that.

CHAPTER FOUR

When the weekend came around, Jason was unsure what he would do. So far he had heard nothing incriminating from Shamus. He had tried leaving Charlie Teddy downstairs to record any conversation, but so far it had only recorded the TV or Maude asking Bradan if he wanted a cup of tea. He still found some of the Irish accent hard to decipher.

"Have you got any plans for the weekend Jason?" Maude asked. "Are you seeing any of your new friends?"

"No, well Gober, you know Gobnait O'Grady, asked if I wanted to go to the library Saturday afternoon with him. I guess I could. It would be something to do."

"Ah that will be fine. He's a good boy. You should hang around with him. Will you not be wanting to play football in the park? Most boys play football at the weekends."

"Um, I don't really like football," Jason said. Shamus walked into the living room and joined in the conversation.

"Don't like football? Is it Rugby you like

better or are you not liking any sports?" Shamus quizzed.

Jason paused before answering. He couldn't tell them about Karate and Judo so he came up with another. "I like swimming. Is there a pool around here with a swimming team?" Jason asked.

"Shankill Swimming pool. They have a club for children and adults. They call themselves the Shankill Sharks. It's on Monday nights. Would you be wanting to go Jason?" Maude asked.

"That place is bloody expensive and full of Royalists. Besides, he has no swim trunks, and you just spent enough money on clothing on him for this month," Shamus said.

"It won't be that much, and I'm sure they will have a pair of trunks in lost property that'll fit the lad. It'll do him good to mix with the likes of Gobnait O'Grady and the kids at the library. I don't want him mixing with the wrong crowd and getting in trouble. The McGinty boys are always in trouble, drive their mother into an early grave they will with worry." Maude said.

*

Jason met Gober at the library on

Saturday. He took out a book he thought he would enjoy, The Secret Seven by Enid Blyton. Gober had already read the whole series and had enjoyed them. The library visit was uneventful, but it got Jason out the house for a few hours. After they left, they said they would catch up with each other on Monday. Jason watched Gober walk and dashed back into the library and picked up the pay phone.

Having no money wasn't a problem. He had a free call number to contact George Young. The call was picked up on the second ring.

"Hello," A voice answered.

"This is Jason Steed." The line went dead for a few moments.

"Jase mate," Scott said.

"Scott." Jason grinned.

"Have you found out where he gets the weapons and bomb making equipment from yet? And have you—" The line went quiet Jason could just hear Scott complaining to someone.

"What's happening?" Jason asked.

"Hello Jason." It was George Young. "Scott should know better than to ask questions like that over the phone. Where can we meet you?"

Jason gave George two possible meeting places, the library on Saturday afternoons or the swimming pool on Monday nights. George said thanks and hung up. At first, Jason was annoyed George hung up so quickly. He wanted to talk to him and Scott. But he realized it was for his own protection. George would not take any chances. The last undercover agent disappeared. Six months later they still hadn't found him or his body.

*

Monday morning felt strange to Jason in a way he hadn't expected. School now seemed familiar. He was no longer the 'New Boy.' Gober waited for him at the gate and walked in with him. A few times Jason had to stop himself from calling him Scott.

After school, Maude took Jason to Shankill swimming pool. He kept back and hid his face in shame while she asked if they had any trunks that would fit her foster son from lost property. He was given a pair of blue trunks. Maude inspected them. "They should fit Jason. They have a pull cord to tighten them. Will you need help?"

"No, I can dress myself okay." He took the shorts and strolled to the men's locker rooms. He looked around and found a corner where the floor was not wet so he wouldn't get his socks wet and quickly changed. The room was full of boys aged eight to fifteen. He looked around the room but never recognized anyone from his school.

Shankill Sharks Youth swimming club was split into three groups. Each group took a section of the pool. They would swim widths in various styles in the groups section. The lower group that occupied the shallow end of the pool was mostly younger swimmers. The middle section was a variety of ages of boys and girls. Being new but able to swim, Jason was first placed in the middle group.

His group instructor barked orders at the group. They first had to dive in and get to the other side with less than two strokes. Later they swam backstroke, front crawl, and breaststroke. Jason found it easy and was soon pulled out of the group and sent to the deep end of the pool to join Coach Gloria and the advanced swimmers.

"They sent me up here," Jason said to the Coach Gloria, a middle age lady wearing a tracksuit that was clearly too small for her.

"Good we need more boys. We have a

competition in two weeks Can you swim the butterfly stroke?" Coach Gloria asked, holding a whistle inches away from her mouth as if it was a microphone.

"Yes, it's not my strongest, but I can," Jason said. He noticed Maude out of the corner of his eye watching him from up in the spectators balcony.

"Well, let's put it to the test." She turned and blew the whistle at the rest of her group. "Cailin Flanagan, I found you a partner for the mixed butterfly relay. I want you two to go to the end of the pool and start swimming widths while I try and get a decent breaststroke pair."

Jason looked at the girl she called Cailin Flanagan. She was very pretty and looked about twelve with dark brown eyes he could just see brown hair poking under her swimming cap. She looked back at Jason. He paused, and with his head slightly tilted, he smiled at her. His brilliant white teeth enticed her; his wet blond hair seductively fell over his wet face.

He knew his smile would attract her. His Grandmother once told him his smile was so handsome it could break any girl's heart, end all wars, and probably cure cancer. Jason just knew he could get a girls attention if he wanted with it. His eyes slightly hidden under his bangs just revealing enough to show off their Sapphire blue color acted like a magnet.

"I'm Cailin who are you?" She asked.

—"Jason, Jason Stee." He paused and corrected himself. "Um. Jason Norris." The pair did as instructed and practiced swimming widths using the butterfly stroke. After a few widths, they both stopped to catch a breath. The brute strength needed to get the technique correct combined with breathing soon sapped their energy. Both Jason and Cailin knew good technique was crucial to swim this style effectively.

"You're quite fast, but you'll need to be when we compete against the Dunmurry Dolphins. They have an Olympic size pool and normally win most of the races against us Sharks." Cailin smiled.

"Dunmurry Dolphins?" Jason asked.

"Yeah the swimming team from Dunmurry. They call themselves that. We are the Shankill Sharks. Are you English?"

"No, I was born in Belfast but went to live in England for a while." Jason's voice faded. He was keen on Cailin and didn't like lying to her.

The next thirty minutes they continued swimming widths. Now and again the group leader shouted at one of them to keep their head up, or push harder, kick harder, and keep ankles together. When the swim was over, they walked along the pool together. An awkward silence and tight-lipped smiles ran across both Cailin and Jason's face.

They paused at the ladies changing room entrance. "So I will see you next Monday?" Cailin asked.

"Sure, I'm looking forward to it, bye," Jason said. He walked to the men's locker rooms with mixed feelings. He was on a mission for George Young, but now he was looking forward to meeting a girl again and entering a pointless swimming competition. He thought he might as well enjoy himself while he was working undercover and do what other boys his age did.

Maude made Jason a hot chocolate to take to bed and passed him Charlie Teddy. "You left him downstairs again this morning. You don't want to be doing that. Suppose Gober came over or that new girl I saw you chatting with from the pool."

"Um, yeah. Habit I guess. When I was

younger I didn't like leaving him alone upstairs so I brought him down. I just grab him when I come down mornings." Jason blushed. He took Charlie and said goodnight to Maude. She stepped forward and kissed his forehead.

"Goodnight, Jason."

Jason struggled to do anything for a moment. Should he have kissed her back? No he was too old. Does a twelve-year-old boy still kiss his mum? He never kissed his father much, just now and again when they had a rare hug. "Thanks for taking me swimming Mrs. O'Neill and..." he paused lost for words. "Well, you know thanks for everything else. Goodnight."

He ran up the stairs. Bradan met him at the top of the stairs. He stood back and let Jason past. He was holding one of his drawings in his hand.

"Goodnight, Bradan," Jason said.

No reply came from Bradan but then again he never did speak. He seemed to keep out of Jason's way and would often leave the room when Jason was around.

Jason lay in bed reflecting the day. He was still awake an hour later. He could hear Shamus downstairs talking and coughing. The television was still on quite loud so he couldn't make out what was said. It gave him an idea. Maybe Charlie Teddy had recorded something.

Jason swung his legs out of bed. The floor felt cold to his bare feet. He picked up Charlie Teddy and took him to bed. He turned his one eye to the left, pushed his nose twice, and listened. Nothing much could be heard again. After fifteen minutes Jason started to doze off. Then, a voice was speaking. He woke instantly and placed Charlie's mouth closer to his ear.

Yes, a man's voice, giving orders. "Use the map I've drawn. These are the look outs. This is where we plant the bomb." Jason's eyes widened. Who was the man speaking? It wasn't Shamus, but Shamus was there. Shamus eventually replied. "Everything would go according to plan."

Jason played it over and over. He couldn't pinpoint whom the other man was, but it was a break-through. Finally, he had something to report to George Young.

CHAPTER FIVE

The walk to school each morning became mundane. The British soldiers stood on some street corners. They looked bored to death. A few made eye contact with Jason and smiled. He found it hard not to smile back. Everyone he mixed with hated them and wanted them out of Northern Ireland except for the Royalists and Unionists. As he was at a predominantly catholic school in an area that was mostly for Independence of Britain, he had to blend in and pretend he loathed them as much as everyone else.

He felt sorry for the soldiers. Some as young as eighteen were just six years older than himself in a place miles away from home and given no thanks for being there. Many soldiers were spat on or cursed at. Some became the targets by local youths who threw stones at them. In many ways, he felt just like them, both believing they were doing something for their country.

*

Friday night he was invited to Gobnait O'Grady's house for dinner after school and to sleep over. The boys would spend Saturday together and go to the library. The O'Grady's home was just like the O'Neill's family home without the stench of cigarettes. Mr. & Mrs. O'Grady went to the social club at eight o'clock to play bingo. Gobnait and Jason were told to go to bed by ten.

Gober surprised Jason as soon as his parents left. "Come on, Jason. Put your coat on; we can go out now."

"Where?" Jason asked.

"Just out. We can go Cherry Knocking," Gober said.

"Um. Okay." Jason never expected Gober of all people to want to play that. He had never played it himself but had heard of it.

They walked a few blocks and Gober spotted the perfect house. "Look, a nice front garden. They have roses and fancy flowers, so they will be old. That's an easy win," Gober said punching the air so hard he could have made a bruise.

Jason stood back and watched while Gober crept up to the front door, rang the bell, clattered the letterbox, and ran back to Jason. Both boys ducked down behind a parked car on the other side of the street, peeking over the hood of the car.

The outside porch light came on and the front door opened. An elderly man with a walking stick came to the door. He looked around and asked "Hello?" several times. Eventually, his elderly wife came out as well and also looked. After a minute or so, they went back inside and the outside light went off. Gober was laughing hysterically. The part of Jason that was still a child wanted to laugh. And the part of Jason that was not a child but a maturing boy thought this was cruel.

"Isn't that cruel, they're really old?" Jason said giving a disapproving look.

"Nah it's awesome. *This* is cruel; watch this," Gober said. He got up and ran back to the house and did the same again. The door opened quicker this time, but Gober had made it back to his hiding spot with Jason. The old man cursed out into the street and threatened to call the police.

Jason looked at Gober. "I don't really find that funny, and I'm surprised you do. I had you down for the quiet nerd type."

"Who are you calling a nerd?"

"I didn't mean anything bad, Gober. I just

don't hang around with trouble makers," Jason said.

Gober looked down on the ground and sighed. "I was trying to impress ya. Show you I'm not a nerd. I like being your friend,. You're tough. You beat Haden McGinty up. I thought you'd like Cherry Knocking."

"Friends don't need to impress each other. Be yourself. What would you normally do on a Friday night? Do you normally sneak out when your parents go out?"

"Yeah, I normally just walk around a bit, watch the older kids at the park; some of them are making out. I just like being out when it's dark. It's exciting and much better than watching the TV," Gober said.

"We can do that, but we don't need to do anything that could get us in trouble with the police. And we don't want to be cruel to old folks." Jason smiled.

Both boys wondered to the park. They watched from a distance some of the older kids acting tough around each other. When they got bored, they went to the pond and threw stones, trying to hit a bottle that was floating in the center. Gober looked at his watch.

"It's nearly ten. We best be getting back."

The boys left Woodvale Park and walked down several small streets when they heard shouting. They rounded a corner and saw Shamus O'Neill drunk, staggering and pointing his finger at two British soldiers.

"You lot needs to get back to bloody Britain. You're not wanted here," Shamus cursed. The two soldiers said nothing. They smiled at him and turned to walk away. "Hey, don't you walk away from me when I'm talking to ya. Do you know who I am?"

They started to walk away, leaving the drunk man in the street cursing at them.

"Isn't that your foster dad;, Shamus?" Gober asked.

Jason embarrassingly nodded. "We better keep out of sight."

Shamus strolled towards the soldiers and pulled one back by his collar. "I'm bloody talking to ya, dirty British pig." The solider tried pulling away. Shamus swung his fist and caught him on the side of his face. The other taller soldier swung a punch at Shamus who saw it coming and ducked and came back with a punch of his own he caught the second soldier on his nose.

Both soldiers fought back, being younger, fitter, and not intoxicated they soon knocked Shamus onto the ground. Once down, they started kicking him, again and again. Shamus curled into a ball and still they kicked him.

"Dirty Irish peasant." One spat and kicked him again and again.

"That's enough. He's hurt, leave him alone," Jason said, striding towards them.

"Clear off kid and mind your own bloody business," The taller soldier said to Jason.

Gober stayed back and watched. Jason moved in between them and Shamus. The simple move to push Jason away was enough for to make him spring into action. He caught the soldier's hand, pulled down on it with a twisting movement, and using the solders weight against him with a judo technique, threw him over his shoulder.

Shamus blinked his eyes and shook his head. He staggered to his feet. The second shorter solider moved quick. He kicked out at Jason. It was blocked. Jason spun on his right leg, his left leg catapulted from his hip and caught the soft flesh of the soldier's stomach. The blow sent him back several feet and winded.

"You filthy pigs will pay for this," Shamus shouted. He had picked up one of the soldier's fallen rifles and aimed it at one.

"No," Jason shouted, standing in the way. "Shamus you can't shoot them."

"Did you see what they did to me? Move out the way boy," Shamus slurred.

Jason threw up his leg in a high kick his foot smashed into Shamus's hand, knocking the rifle clean away. Both soldiers had recovered and now a rifle was aimed at Shamus and Jason.

"See what you did now, you Eejit," Shamus cursed at Jason.

"He's drunk sorry. He shouldn't have touched you, but you shouldn't have kicked him and kept kicking him and then tried hurting me. No one got hurt; let me take him home. Sorry for the trouble," Jason said, passing them the other rifle.

"No, son, he's under arrest," the solider said, moving forward.

"Do you *really* want to arrest him and inform your superiors that you tried hitting a kid and he got your guns off you? That won't look good for you guys will it? Let me take him home.

You go on your way," Jason said he walked forward and faced them.

Both soldiers looked at each other puzzled. The kid was making sense. The situation was awkward for them, plus this boy spoke with an English accent and seemed to be almost giving them an order. They were obviously unsure what to do. They looked at each other, hoping one would give a reply.

Jason turned to Shamus. "I'll take you home." Gober had finally come out of hiding. They walked Shamus home. When he got to the front door, he stopped and supported himself up against it and studied Jason.

"Don't ever get between me and a British pig again. What the hell are you two doing out anyway?" Shamus said, trying to pull his sleeve back to check his watch.

"Um," Jason said. "We were at the park."

"Who taught you to fight like that, back there you?" He paused, still trying to pull his sleeve back and steady himself against the door. "You took down two soldiers?" Shamus asked scratching his head.

"You had already hit them Shamus. I just kicked one and the other tripped over me," Jason said.

"Well on this occasion, I won't say nothing to Maude, but you two better be getting to bed. If you're still staying at Gobnait's house you better get," Shamus slurred and pointed away and to the sky.

*

Jason was sleeping on a pullout mattress in Gobers room. They never said much until they climbed into their beds. Gober's older brother Liam O'Grady was already asleep in his bunk.

"How *did* you learn to fight? That solider never tripped over you. That was a judo throw and that kick you did on the other was well, pretty awesome. It knocked him back clean across the street. They were adults, and you didn't even break a sweat. Then you disarmed Shamus," Gober whispered.

"I don't like to mention it so keep it to yourself else everyone will want to test me. I've had a couple of karate lessons and some judo," Jason said. He failed to mention he was a black belt in Judo. and three disciplines of Karate. And at the age of ten, he was the under sixteen Hong Kong karate Champion.

"A *couple*. I think a few more than that.

Why keep that a secret?"

"If people at school knew I did a bit, they would all want to try and fight me so I keep it to myself."

"So that's how you beat Haden McGinty."

"Good night mate." Jason yawned, trying to change the subject.

"Will you two shut it?" Liam cursed and swung his pillow at Gober. "I was asleep. And your new friend better not snore, or I'll take it out on you."

"Sorry," both Gober and Jason said simultaneously.

CHAPTER SIX

Jason slept surprisingly well on the spare mattress. Although Liam made sure he woke both Jason and Gober up when he got up at six to go and do his morning paper route. The fourteen-year-old let his alarm ring and ring even after he climbed out of bed, and he gave Jason's mattress a kick for good measure.

Gober and Jason went to the library as before. Jason noticed Scott peeking between the bookshelves. Jason pretended to be looking for a new book and joined Scott.

"Hi Mate," Scott beamed.

"Scott, hi I have some news. The teddy bear picked it up," Jason said. He reported to Scott what happened and told him about the incident with the two soldiers. He wasn't sure if Shamus would have actually shot them or not but didn't want to find out.

"What's it like staying at the base?" Jason asked.

"It's so boring. The soldiers march around the parade ground, workout in the gym, and march some more. Although, they do talk about girls a lot and have a large supply of adult magazines." Scott grinned. "Hurry up and solve this mission. I'm bored to death. What's the mixed school like?"

"The school's okay. I'm practically top in every subject. I have to hold back on French; I think I know more than the teacher. Oh, but I got to tell you this, it's so funny. In Math class the teacher, a Mr. Griggs, was showing us how to add and subtract fractions. I almost died laughing when he said in his strong Irish accent 'what is two times tree and tree turds?'" Jason laughed. "I was like, what did he say? Did he mean three and three thirds?"

Scott burst out laughing. "No way."

"Yeah he did and then every time he should have said a third he said a turd. My stomach was hurting I was laughing so much. The Irish accent is so funny sometimes and no one else was laughing. Tt's normal to them. I was hoping he would pick me for an answer so I could say for example one and one turd." Jason laughed out loud.

"Shush," the librarian said from the front desk, giving both Scott and Jason a dirty look.

"Apart from that, school is fine, and some of the girls are pretty hot," Jason said in a quieter voice.

"Girls, what about Catherine? You can't be looking at girls," Scott teased.

"Catherine and I are just good friends now, besides I'm just looking." Jason smiled.

"Who's the bookworm?" Scott asked, his head nodded towards Gober.

"Oh that's my friend, Gobnait O'Grady."

"*Gobnait?* No way they called a kid that." Scott laughed.

"Shush boys, this is a library," the female librarian said as she approached.

Jason turned red. His fingers danced across the book covers. Gober looked up and put his head back into his book. He gave Scott the small amount of information he had heard from Charlie regarding the bomb. Scott and Jason whispered goodbye to each other. Scott would meet him at the swimming pool Monday night to see if he had any more information.

Gober never mentioned Jason getting told to be quiet in the library and talking to another boy. Jason thought George Young was right to use Scott at his contact. No one would suspect two boys the same age chatting.

*

On Sunday, Jason went home to the O'Neill's in the afternoon. After lunch, Maude said she would take him with her to visit her sister. Just before they left, Jason brought Charlie Teddy down stairs again, hid him under a chair, and turned him on recording.

Maude's sister was excited to see Maude with her new foster child. Jason had to sit through an afternoon of woman's chatter while her husband sat watching cricket. Jason could never remember being so bored in all his life.

When they arrived home in the evening, Shamus and Bradan were out, but Jason noticed the house smelt worse than ever of tobacco smoke and the ashtrays were full of cigarette butts. That night, he took Charlie to bed and replayed the tape. As expected, a group of men were talking. He could pick out Shamus and the voice he heard before. He seemed to be in charge of the group and giving orders. Jason knew he had to find out who that man was. This had to be the top man in the IRA.

Another new breakthrough came. They kept referring to 'SS.' Shamus himself said he would be meeting 'SS' next Wednesday. The strangers voice again took charge of the meeting and discussed an ambush. Jason could just hear a rustle of paper; they were using a map. He needed to find the map and get it to George Young.

*

He walked faster than normal to swimming practice. He was going on his own. He felt excited and wasn't sure if it was because he had news to pass onto Scott or he was seeing Cailin Flanagan again.

Both Jason and Cailin practiced the butterfly stroke non-stop. They were recording faster times and where told they had a good chance of winning at the swimming competition next weekend. The whole swim team was excited and looking forward to next week's competition.

"Jason it's my thirteenth birthday next Saturday. After the swimming competition, my parents are giving me a small party at the house. Nothing big, just party food. My brother has a friend who is a DJ and he is bringing his equipment over so we will have some music," Cailin announced.

"Sounds nice, are you inviting me?" Jason asked.

Cailin looked awkward. She took off her

swimming cap and let her hair fall down. "If you want to come," she said, not making eye contact.

"I'd love to come." Jason smiled. She grinned back at him. He watched her walk off to the ladies locker rooms.

Jason met Scott in the men's locker room. It was packed with boys getting changed. No one gave Scott a second glance. Jason rinsed off in the shower and beckoned Scott into the corner of the changing area with him.

"Hi, Jase. You look like you were really into that swimming," Scott said.

"Were you watching?" Jason asked.

"Yeah, I was up in the spectator's balcony. Although, you probably didn't see me your eyes were fixed on that girl you were with. She's quite hot," Scott said.

Jason took off his wet trunks and threw them at Scott, catching him on the face.

"Eeewww that's wet and nasty. You better not have peed in them," Scott complained.

Jason laughed and dried himself. "She's called Cailin Flanagan, I got invited to her birthday party Saturday. I agreed to go, of course *only* just to spy on them and find more info."

"Yeah right. The only info you want from her is can you make out with her or not," Scott said.

"Well, I have to do something. Being a spy is so boring sometimes. This mission is hard work because it's boring. Give me assassins, crocodiles, leopards, and helicopter gunships, but don't give me another Sunday afternoon at Maude's sisters house. I seriously thought I was gonna die of Boredamnesia".

"*Boredamnesia?* Is that even a word?" Scott laughed, wringing his friend's trunks out for him.

"It is now. Boredamnesia means you spent Sunday afternoon with someone's family and you were forced to listen to Irish woman gossip and watch cricket at the same time on a black and white TV," Jason said, pulling on his clothing. "But I have some news."

Jason passed the information to Scott. They both agreed the 'SS' initials could be anyone's, but Scott said he would work on it and let George know everything. They both agreed they needed the map the men were looking at, and Jason had to find out who the other voice was on Charlie Teddy's tape.

*

Another week passed quickly and Jason had no new information to pass on. The O'Neill house had been quiet. The one thing that kept Jason absorbed was the swimming competition on Saturday and Cailin's Birthday party after. Maude agreed to buy a box of chocolates for her and a card. Jason sat at the kitchen table writing it out. He was unsure whether to sign it from Jason or love from Jason. In the end, he just wrote Jason and put a small 'x' underneath.

"So Jason, Maude tells me we have to go to the pool tonight to watch you in a swimming competition?" Shamus said, sitting down heavily next to Jason.

"You don't have to come," Jason said, licking the envelope shut.

"Sure we do. We want to cheer you on, and I hear you are going to a birthday party after. It was a young lass that asked you?"

"Yeah, Cailin. She's my swimming partner and friend."

"Friend, nonsense. Gober's your friend. This girl Cailin, she must be something special?" Shamus teased.

Jason colored up. He was unsure how he felt about her and tried not to get too close. He knew once the mission was over he would be leaving Ireland.

"What's her full name. Do we know her family, Maude?" Shamus asked.

"I don't know," Maude said. She was serving up egg and chips.

"Cailin Flanagan," Jason said.

Both Maude, Bradan, and Shamus all looked at each other. Jason immediately picked up on it.

"Is that a problem?" Jason asked slowly.

"Are you telling me I spent *my* money on a card and chocolates for a Flanagan?" Shamus shouted.

"Shamus, we don't know if she its *his* daughter. Flanagan is a popular name," Maude said.

"Have you seen her father?" Shamus questioned Jason, his eyes almost popping out of his head.

"Um. Yeah, not to speak too. Is

something wrong?" Jason asked.

"What does he look like? What does he do for a job?" Shamus asked.

"Tall guy, white hair, and he wears a dog collar, so maybe a vicar or minister," Jason said.

Shamus slammed his hand on the table and cursed. "I told you Maude, he shouldn't have gone to Shankill pool. It's full of bloody Unionists and now Jason is gooey-eyed over that bloody Reverend Ian Flanagan's daughter. Well that's that. You won't be going swimming or to her party."

"Shamus, they're just kids," Maude said.

"I'm entered in the butterfly stroke. I have to go. The team is relying on me," Jason argued.

Shamus bent down and faced Jason, his nose just inches away from Jason's. "No. We don't have anything to do with them. They are giving away our country to the Brits, and that bloody Reverend Ian Flanagan is a spokesman and leader of the Unionist party. No son of mine will be seen dead in his house."

Jason forgot himself his short temper ignited. "I'm not your son, and I don't care about your politics and religion or his."

Shamus punched Jason and caught the side of his face, knocking him back and onto the floor. Jason never expected it and didn't have time to block the blow.

"Shamus," Maude screamed. "You can't hit him. He's just a boy."

Jason sprang to his feet. His pupils darkened as he forced adrenaline into his system. He shook, trying to control his temper and hold himself back. Shamus came closer for more. Much to Jason's surprise, Bradan caught Shamus by the arm and pulled him back.

"Say sorry to the boy," Bradan said, keeping a firm grip on his brother's arm, glaring at Shamus.

Jason was stunned. He had never heard him talk before, but more so because he recognized his voice. He was the voice on Charlie Teddy's tape.

Shamus nodded and looked at Jason. "I'm sorry I smacked you Jason. I have no excuse."

"You didn't smack me you *punched* me," Jason argued rubbing his cheek.

"Shamus, in the name of Jesus, are ye crazy? Maude loves the kid and even I've got used to having him around now. He's a good kid," Bradan said in his heavy Irish brogue.

Maude was sobbing. She put her arm around Jason and tried to hug him. He was stiff and still ready to fight.

"Jason please don't mention this to anyone. He never meant to do that. They will take you away," Maude sobbed.

"Sorry, Jason. Look, for Maude's sake and Bradan's, and well even mine, please can you forgive me? You can go swimming and to the party. I can't help myself sometimes. I hate the British and Unionists. Flanagan is head of the Unionist party. Sorry I just lost it."

Jason said nothing; he turned towards Maude and hugged her back. He couldn't help but like her. He knew if he was to say something to the authorities and get moved now it would mean all this time had gone to waste. Plus, he was so close to finding out who 'SS' was.

"It's just a birthday party Shamus," Jason said. "Sorry for arguing with you and what I said about me not being your son. I like living here, and I do think of you as my dad."

"I know. I over reacted. Let's have some food," Shamus said, shaking Jason's hand.

Jason looked at Bradan and raised his eyebrows. It was a look he inherited from his father. Scott called it the 'Steed asking a question look!' and in this case, like in most it worked.

Bradan sighed. "I guess I owe you an explanation. I have an important job. I help to defend my country. The British, with the help of the Unionists like your new girlfriend's father, want to keep us part of Britain and ruled by the British Government five hundred miles away and that stuck up royal family. They will stop at nothing to silence us. Many think I'm retarded or slow. I'm not. It's my cover not many know about. Only very close friends and family. I now consider you as the later."

"I didn't think you liked me?" Jason asked.

"To start with, I didn't give a shite about ya and your English accent didn't help you much either laddie. But as I noticed how happy you made Maude and I heard how you looked after Shamus when the Eejit got drunk and tried to fight two armed soldiers, well, you kind of grew on me. Although, you're as nutty as a fruitcake. You do all that and you fought a McGinty in school and just stood up to Shamus ready to fight. Then on the other hand, you sleep with a teddy bear." Bradan smiled.

Jason smiled back and shrugged his

shoulders. "We all have secrets." He wouldn't admit it, but he liked Bradan.

*

Whenever there was a game or match or contest of any sort between the residents of Shankill and Dunmurry, the tensions were higher, the crowds were bigger, and things just seemed more important.

The Shankill Sharks stood in a line on one side of the pool, while the Dunmurry Dolphins stood the other side. Cailin worked her way towards Jason and stood next to him. As expected, the Dunmurry Dolphins were winning most of the events. The total score was seventeen wins to the Dolphins and just two for the Sharks. Most of the Sharks along, with their parents and followers, were now depressed and acknowledged they had lost yet again.

"Is there any point us racing? Even if we win our doubles race, our team has still lost and look who we are up against," Cailin whispered to Jason. He looked over at the opposition, a boy aged about fifteen and a girl of similar age. "They *have* to be almost sixteen. How can we beat them?"

"We will beat them, oh. Happy Birthday." He smiled. "Just concentrate on the style. I want you to go first," Jason said.

"Coach said you had to swim the first two lengths as you are fastest to try and give us a lead. The swimmer against me will be in my wake," Cailin said.

"Cailin you go first, give it everything you have. I will take the last two lengths."

Maude and Shamus watched from the balcony. Shamus looked at the rest of the Shark spectators, and just a few seats away, he eyed the Reverend Ian Flanagan with hatred in his eyes. Flanagan too had noticed Shamus. If looks could kill, Shamus would now be a dead man.

The mixed pairs' butterfly stroke race was the last event. Both teams were called to the start line. Cailin did as Jason told her and went to the edge. The other team were clearly older than her and Jason. The older girl tied her hair up in her swimming cap and sneered at Cailin.

The boy looked down at Jason. "Good luck, you're gonna need it," He said smugly. "You could save yourself the trouble of getting your long hair wet and just give up now."

Shankill Sharks coach looked annoyed. She had wanted Jason to swim the first two lengths and couldn't understand why Cailin was going first.

"On your mark," a judge bellowed, raising his hand and holding a whistle inches from his mouth. Both the tall girl and Cailin approached the edge and bent forward into diving position with toes just curled over the edge.

"It's not fair. That pair is much bigger and older than our Jason and his partner," Maude complained to Shamus.

The whistle blew. The two girls dived long and deep into the pool, both performing a dolphin kick. It was clear by just over half way the Dunmurry Dolphin team were going to win. Cailin fought back, but by the time she turned her taller opponent was starting her final length.

Rev Ian Flanagan stood and shouted. "Come on Sharks! Come on Cailin, you can catch her."

Jason had only used his ability to induce adrenaline into his system when he had to defend himself. Wong Tong, his karate master, taught him the ancient Chinese art. Jason could bring it on but only used it if he was in danger. The adrenaline rush would give him a burst of energy, power that can only come when you really needed it. The side effect was severe fatigue. His young body's blood sugar was burnt, and he was often exhausted to the point of almost collapse.

Taking deep breaths, Jason concentrated. The cheers and shouts of encouragement to the two girls were completely blocked out. Jason could hear just his heartbeat. His pupils dilated. His body trembled, adrenaline flushing through his body, his muscle fibers twitching as they recoiled, ready to spring into action.

The opposing team had a huge lead. The taller girl hit the edge of the wall. It was the signal for her partner to go. He dived high and long, going deep, kicking hard. Moments later, Cailin gave a final burst and touched the side. Jason's powerful legs forced his light body off the side in a perfect dive. His legs kicked and his arms took a stroke under water. The second kick and Jason broke the surface of the water.

He sucked in a large breath of air, filling his lungs before going down again. Forcing himself faster and faster, his arms pounded the water's surface and with perfect harmony with his powerful legs kicking forcing his body through the water. He approached the end of the pool and went down to turn. He pushed off from the side and broke though the water's surface.

Screams echoed throughout the pool of encouragement. Jason had caught up with the taller boy who glanced across and noticed the younger smaller boy level with him. His pride was not going to let this little blond haired boy beat him. He fought back, his larger legs and powerful arms smashing through the water.

Rev Ian Flanagan had stepped to the railings on the balcony and cheered. "Go Sharks, go sharks, go boy go." A man stood next to him equally excited and screaming at the top of his lungs.

"Jason go, go on boy keep going you got it, go on," Shamus shouted, punching the air with his fist. A few spectators had to take a second look. Shamus O'Neill and Rev Ian Flanagan were side by side, leaning over the balcony and cheering for the same team.

Jason was still level with his opponent. Who was winning was too close to call. Sharks. Jason imagined a shark in real life or the crocodile that almost ate him alive. It was chasing him, trying to get his feet. He imagined it chasing him. he had to get out of the water and quick. The last few strokes Jason stayed under. He never climbed to get a full breath. His final spurt of speed gave him a small lead.

The screaming and cheers were deafening around the entire complex. Maude had tears in her eyes, her voice hoarse from shouting encouragement.

"Go go go boy," shouted Rev Flanagan.

Jason's hand hit the edge of the pool a second before the Dunmurry boy's hand. The judge raised his hand. Jason and Cailin had won. Rev Flanagan and Shamus cheered and raised their hands. They both high fived each other and then realized who the other person was. They stopped and looked at each other; despite the deep hatred for each other, they couldn't help but smile at one another before returning to their seats.

Jason lost his grip on the side of the pool and went under. He fought back to catch the edge but missed and went under again. He kicked up and coughed trying to get air. Cailin noticed dropped her towel and jumped in and caught him, lifting his head out of the water. He has swallowed a mouthful of water. His body was exhausted, his oxygen level dangerously low. She held him and called for help.

The judge, a heavy set man, bent down and pulled Jason out and lay him on the ground. Jason coughed up a mouthful of water. His lungs heaved, trying collect needed oxygen.

"Jason," Maude screamed. The other swimmers surrounded him. The coach lifted him to his feet. Jason's eyes were still dark and unresponsive. Cailin was worried as she stroked his forehead.

Shamus ran down the stairs and made his way to the scene. He was relieved to see Jason was up on his feet with a towel around him. He was nodding at the coach.

"I'm fine, just over did it," Jason panted.

"Are you all right boy?" Shamus asked.

Jason nodded.

The Shankill Sharks still lost seventeen races and only won three, but because of the thrilling final race and the way Jason caught up, you could have been mistaken and thought they had won the entire competition.

Jason and Cailin collected a small medal. Rev Flanagan took a picture of the pair together holding their medals.

"My parents will drive you to our home, see you outside?" Cailin said. Jason nodded. He wasn't fully recovered and unsteady on his feet.

Shamus put his arm around him and walked him to the men's locker rooms. "Are you sure you're okay to go still?"

"You said I could go," Jason whined.

"Yes you can son. I'm just worried about ya. You look spaced out."

Jason sighed. "That took a lot out of me. I will be okay when I have something to eat." He leant against Shamus for support.

Shamus helped Jason get dressed and waited while he fussed with his hair. "Okay laddie, lets go."

"My hair isn't right. I should have washed it. The chlorine makes it look greasy."

"Are you a boy or a girl? Who bloody cares about your hair?" Shamus paused. "Okay of course you want to look handsome for that girl. Cailin is it?"

"Yeah Cailin." Jason smiled. "Her parents are going to give me a ride to her house."

"I see, then you won't be needing me and Maude."

Jason looked and felt guilty.

"Ha I'm only joking laddie. You go and have a good time. Besides, I have an important job to do tonight." Shamus smiled.

Jason waited outside the pool entrance for

Cailin. He noticed her coming with her father and who he assumed was her mother. He greeted her with a smile.

"Jason, you look different. I guess I haven't seen you with your clothes on before," Cailin said. "Oh that didn't come out right, did it?" She laughed.

"I was going to say the same to you, but I assume this is your mom, so thought better of it. Pleased to meet you., Jason said shaking Cailin's mum's hand. She gave Jason a firm handshake. Her hair was unnaturally black. Jason noticed the roots were grey, but she had a welcoming smile and he took an instant liking to her.

Jason climbed in the back of the Flanagan's car with Cailin. He noticed her long brown hair. He had never seen it before. It was always hidden under her swim cap. "I never knew you had long hair."

"Do you like it?" Cailin asked.

"Yes of course, you look…" He paused. He noticed Cailin's father looking at him in the drivers mirror. It made him feel uneasy saying what was on his mind. "Um, nice with it."

CHAPTER SEVEN

Cailin's party was nothing like he had expected. Her sixteen-year-old brother Niall was there. Cailin's parents and her grandmother as well. Her mother had made sandwiches, cake, chicken wings, and sausages on sticks.

They sat around a large table and waited for her father to join them. He sat and smiled at Jason.

"Jason, as you're our guest, please do us the honor and say grace," Rev Flanagan asked. Immediately before Jason could answer or make an excuse, the family all bowed their heads.

Jason turned bright red. He had never been taught to say grace. He had attended church with the Sea Cadets for special Sunday parades, but being raised by nannies in Hong Kong, religion was never pushed on him. He had heard some say grace while he was at the Military School in the United States and when at his grandparents though.

"Um…" he stammered. "Em, well um. Thank you for bringing us together tonight for Cailin's Birthday and um, thanks for the food we have here." He paused again. "And most importantly, thank you for bringing my step father Shamus O'Neill and Reverend Flanagan together tonight. Amen." Jason's face was flushed. He hated speaking publicly, even a small group was hard for him. He instinctively pulled his blond bangs over his eyes.

Cailin smiled at him and looked at her father. "Yes dad. I heard you and Shamus O'Neill shook hands tonight."

"Nothing of the sort. That man is a complete." He stopped himself. "I will keep my feelings to myself. Tonight was not about the Irish Republicans or the Unionists; it was about you two at a sports event. Don't read too much into it. We are as far apart on politics as the North Pole is away from the South Pole."

"Shamus O'Neill is your foster father?" Niall asked Jason. "No way."

"Yes."

"Are you trying to give dad a heart attack, Cailin, bringing his son home here?" Niall laughed.

"I didn't know who Jason lived with. Besides, Jason is my friend, and who he lives with has nothing to do with you." Cailin screwed her eyes up at her brother and pulled a face.

"Just thought you would have been more considerate," Niall said smugly.

"If you ever had a girlfriend I would never say anything, no matter if she was any color or religion, but no girl in her right mind would ever date an ugly Gobshite like you," Cailin said.

"Now, now you two. We have a guest, and he *is* very welcome here," Rev Flanagan interrupted.

After they had eaten and pretended to laugh at Niall's jokes, Cailin asked if she could take Jason up to her room to play some music.

Jason smiled when he entered her room. He took in his surroundings. She had a David Cassidy poster on one wall above her bed and a large poster of a cute looking lamb and calf. The message underneath read 'Don't Eat Me.' Another of some cute piglets wearing bowties had the same message.

"You don't eat meat?" Jason asked.

"No, I don't. Why would I want to eat dead animal flesh?"

"Em, so you never ate any of the chicken or sausages on sticks?" he asked.

"No yuk, that's nasty. I ate the cheese sandwiches and the cheese and pickle. It's just me the rest of my family all eat *dead animals.*"

"Are you trying to make me feel guilty for eating meat?"

"Yep." She smiled at him and sat on the bed.

"If we're not supposed to eat animals then why are they made of meat?" Jason grinned and joined her. He flicked his blond fringe away from his eyes and stared at her. Their eyes locked simultaneously their faces moved closer. She looked into his sapphire blue eyes. His blond eyebrows stood out against his lightly tanned face.

Jason's eyes lowered to her lips. He could feel her breath on his face. *Is it too soon to kiss her?* he asked himself. His body leaned forward, forcing his face closer. He needed to kiss her. She was beautiful. He tilted his face slightly and moved forward. He closed his eyes.

"Cailin, Mum asked what time Jason has to be home?" Niall asked, standing at the doorway. Jason and Cailin turned and faced him. "Oh sorry, did I interrupt something?"

Jason sprung to his feet. "No we were just talking. As it's a school night, I have to be home by nine," he said, turning bright red.

"Mum will drive you home. I'll let her know." Niall grinned at his sister. "Carry on, Sis."

Cailin and Jason both blushed at each other and said nothing for a few minutes. Jason spotted a notepad on her dresser. It had the word "Jason" written on it in large letters. Each letter was colored in a different color. A large heart was drawn below his name. It gave him the courage to ask "Do you want to go to the movies Saturday afternoon?" There was a charming nervousness in his voice.

"Is that like we are going on a date?" Cailin asked.

The question was not what he expected. Of course it's a date, he thought to himself, but had second thoughts. "Um, I normally hang out with a mate Saturday's, he's called Gober, well Gobnait, but we call him Gober. If you have a friend maybe the four of us could go. Oh there is one small problem."

"Yes, I will ask Megan she's my best friend. What's the small problem?" Cailin asked.

"I don't have any money, I can see if Maude, she's my foster mum, will let me have some but not enough for everyone, sorry."

"That's not a problem Jason. You just bring Gober and we will have a good time. I will find out what they are showing," Cailin said. They both walked down the stairs together.

"George, it's no wonder you're fat. Look at what you just ate." Scott laughed.

George burped and stared at Scott. "For someone with so many IQ points, what is it 168—?"

"174 now," Scott interrupted.

"For someone with so much brains, you say the stupidest of things sometimes. 'Ere we are on a Saturday night, just had a good dinner at one of Belfast's finest restaurants, good conversation with someone I considered a friend, and you go and spoil it. You have no tact." George burped again. "Now Jason has a little more tact than you. He just has a temper that I fear will get him into serious trouble one day."

"I'm just honest. Besides, it's a known fact men over forty-five who are overweight have fifty four point three percent more chance of having a heart attack," Scott said.

"See there you bloody go again. You

almost put me off ordering desert," George said, shaking his head.

"*Almost*, you're not seriously going to eat more?" Scott laughed.

"I hear the Irish cream chocolate cake they do here is the best in the land. Gotta try it now we are here," George said. Scott smiled back at him. The two had been staying at the army barracks for weeks while Jason was undercover. Most evenings George took Scott out to dinner at various eating establishments. It gave them both a break from the barracks and a chance to discover Belfast. George was also allowed to put it on expenses, so that helped.

"I'll be glad to get back to England. This has to be the most boring mission ever. I thought helping out as a spy would be exciting," Scott said.

"It's not like James Bond," George said. Besides, you've been out and met up with Jason a few times and collected some information under the eyes of our suspects."

"Hardly cloak and dagger stuff. Once in a library and we both got told off by a librarian and the other time in the men's locker rooms surrounded by naked wet guys while Jason dressed," Scott said faking a yawn. "But if it makes you feel better, George, I won't call you fat again. You're not fat, just easier to see than most." Scott grinned.

*

After the birthday party, Cailin's mum drove Jason back to the O'Neill's house. Cailin came for the ride. The young couple sat in the back of the car together. When the car took a turn, Cailin put her hand down to stop herself sliding in the seat. Her hand landed on Jason's. She left it there for a moment. When she took it away, Jason took it and held it. They looked at each other and smiled.

"This is it here, the house with the red door and all the empty milk bottles outside," Jason said.

"Oh my you do get through a lot of milk," Cailins mum said.

When the car stopped, he opened the back door. "Thank you for having me, Mrs. Flanagan." He looked at Cailin. "Bye Cailin, see you Saturday?"

"Yes bye Jason. I'll phone you," Cailin said. They looked at each other. Jason heard Maude open the front door. Cailin's mum watched them in her driver's mirror. He wanted to kiss her goodbye, but too many eyes were watching, and it would be their first kiss. He didn't want to ruin it. He gave her hand a gentle squeeze before letting go and climbed out. He waved them off and almost skipped into the house.

Maude stopped in the hallway and looked at him. "And what's that on your face?" she asked.

Jason felt his face, he checked in the small mirror that hung in the hall. "What? I can't see anything."

"With your eyes shining like that and the biggest smile I have ever seen, I would call it a love struck face."

"No, it's the chlorine from the pool. It stung my eyes." He grinned.

"How are you feeling? We were worried about you Jason. You over did it in that race."

"As you can see, I'm fine, but I'm tired. I'll go to bed now, goodnight," Jason said. He leant forward and gave Maude a hug. It was a small brief hug. To Jason, it was just being nice, and he was in a great mood. To Maude, it meant the world.

"Oh here, you left your teddy bear down here again. Unless now you are all grown up and have a girlfriend you won't be needing him..." Maude teased.

Jason grabbed Charlie Teddy and ran up the stairs two at a time to bed. He wasn't sure where his friendship with Cailin was going, but it felt right and helped beat the boredom of the mission.

He turned out his light and jumped into bed. His eyes were heavy, his body still tired from his exhausting swim. He turned to sleep and noticed Charlie Teddy. He picked him up and turned him on and placed Charlie's mouth by his ear.

This should send me to sleep, Jason said to himself, not expecting anything. He listened for ten minutes and fought off the sleep that called him. He could hear the TV in the background and the theme of the five o'clock news. Jason assumed this was just after he left and doubted he would hear anything as Shamus and Maude left not long after to attend the swimming event.

He could clearly hear Bradan and Shamus talking. "He's head of SYUI. George Young he's called. You can't miss him, big fat guy. He goes out every night around seven thirty with his kid for dinner. The kids about thirteen and apparently a nerdy looking thing. George Young wears the same black suit. If he's here, it can't be good for us. If we take him out it will be a boost of confidence for our supporters and show the bloody Brits we mean business. I have someone following him. He will pass the word of where the fat English pig is eating. It's normally around nine thirty. And when he comes out. Pop."

Jason sat up. He couldn't believe his ears. It was Bradan talking. He looked at his alarm clock, its luminous hands telling him it was almost nine twenty. "Shamus said he had something to do tonight," Jason said under his breath, changing from his pajamas into his clothing as fast as he could.

He sneaked down the stairs. Maude was in the living room watching TV. He gently lifted the phone and dialed the number he was given. After several rings and no answer, panic started to set in. He had to warn George. He dropped the phone down before he grabbed his coat and snuck out the front door.

He ran at the same time zipping up his coat as he left. The night air was very cold, reminding him that winter was on its way. The more he thought about the message, the faster he ran. He sprinted down the street and cut across the park, running as quickly as he could.

The park was silent. The moon had risen and the air was still. The park was caught up in a pale buttery light. The grass and earth beneath his feet seemed to throb with peace, and from above came light from heavens older than man. He had made it halfway across the park playing field.

His silent solitude came to an abrupt end when a pair of headlamps came on. A van, Jason guessed. It was parked on the other side of the park, although blinding the lights gave him the direction of Main Street. He would follow that up into the town and hope to spot Shamus or George.

Two figures or was it three climbed out of the van. It was hard for Jason to say exactly. They were protected by the bright lights that shone in his direction. As he got closer he counted four men.

"What's the hurry sonny?" one called out. Jason ignored him and kept running albeit in his direction. Two moved forward to block Jason's path. He slowed down and tried walking fast.

"I asked a question. Now where would a kid your age be going at night and so fast?" the man asked again.

"I'm not supposed to talk to strangers. I'm going home," Jason said. He noticed the other two. They were both carrying what looked like baseball bats.

"We are not strangers, kid. We clean up the area, make sure no one is breaking the law," The man barked as he paced towards Jason. "What's your name laddie and where do you live?"

Jason stopped and took in his surroundings. Four men, two carrying baseball bats. "Creggan Cleaners?" Jason asked.

"Smart kid." The man smiled and looked at the others. "Then you know you had better answer our questions."

"I'm going home, and I'm late. That's why I was running," Jason said.

"And where do you live?"

"I can't tell you that. I don't know you."

"You don't get a choice. I want your name address and what school you go to? If I have to ask again, I'll make you sorry." He was a few feet from Jason. His threat angered Jason. He was thinking about what Shamus had told him. The Creggan Cleaners had kneecapped Haden McGinty's brother because he was stealing cars and stole from an old lady. Although Jason felt

McGinty was wrong, he should have been brought to justice by the police. These men where nothing more than thugs themselves playing at being police.

"No, I don't talk to strangers. I have to go. We are on the same side, although I don't shoot kids' kneecaps so they spend their life in a wheelchair." Jason raised himself on his toes as they approached.

"Who the bloody hell do ya think you are talking to?" The man cursed, raising his hand.

"Oh big man, gonna hit a twelve-year-old kid now? What's next, chop off the fingers of anyone who doesn't flush the toilet properly or clean their teeth?" Jason said.

The four men looked at each other, unsure what to do next.

"You need a good walloping. If I ever spoke to my old man like that—" he was interrupted.

"You're not my old man. You're a bully threatening a kid who just wants to get home. Now can I go now please?" Jason said. He tried to walk away. One made a grab for him. Jason blocked his hand and twisted it, pulling it down. For good measure he kicked the man in the groin.

"Ah you little, Git," the man screamed, falling to his knees.

Jason ran at another man. At the last second, he ducked and ran passed, sprinting away, closely followed by two of them on foot. His pursuers where overweight smokers. Despite their larger, legs Jason was fast, extremely fit, and desperate to find George and Scott. He took one corner at the end of the park into the busy Belfast Street and had lost his pursuers. The cold air sliced him as he fled; his chest was like an oven that burned and stung when he gasped it in and then set off a burning sensation across his chest. He swallowed salvia, trying to ease the burning.

CHAPTER EIGHT

Jason ran street after street. Every restaurant he came to he went and looked for George. He turned down Howard Street and had to stop at a pay phone. He called the number he was given again. After five rings and no answer, he slammed down the receiver in anger and set off running again, not exactly sure where he was running, just going to each restaurant and trying to find George and Scott.

*

Three men sat nervously outside the Shaw Restaurant, the famed Belfast restaurant named after Irish Playwright George Bernard Shaw. He often played host to celebrities when visiting Belfast.

Shamus O'Neill checked his American made Smith and Wesson .38 special for the hundredth time. He noticed movement at the exit of the restaurant. He pulled a black knitted hood over his head; it had two round holes cut out for his eyes.

*

George Young and Scott Turner were just

leaving Shaw Steakhouse.

"Looks cold outside," Scott said, zipping up his coat and tucking his hands in his pockets.

"You kids are bloody soft. This ain't cold. When I was a kid, it was so bloody cold the only thing that kept us kids warm was my mother's love," George said.

"Is that back when you lived in a cave afraid to go out because a dinosaur would eat you?" Scott replied.

The two stepped out onto the pavement and walked towards the car. Jason looked down the street. The familiar round shape of George Young was impossible to confuse even for a bat. He started jogging towards them. Scott looked up, trying to make out who the boy was running towards them.

"Is that Jason coming?" Scott asked George.

George looked down the street.

"George Young is it?" Shamus called. George looked to his right. A tall hooded man stood still in the road watching him.

"Who's asking?" George said. He

immediately suspected something was wrong and yanked Scott back by his neck and shielded him behind him.

"Tiocfaidh ár lá." Shamus shouted the Irish phrase meaning *Our day will come* as he raised his trembling hand. George threw himself on top of Scott. Jason could see the gunman in the distance and ran as fast as he could. Two shots rang out. Then another. George coughed and collapsed, crushing Scott.

Shamus ran back to the waiting car and jumped in the back door. The wheels screeched as it sped off away from the murder scene. George never moved. People in the nearby restaurant stayed inside. No one ventured outside. A few braver or inquisitive kept low and looked out the windows.

"George," Jason shouted as he approached. He noticed Scott's legs underneath George. A large pool of blood was forming. "Scott."

Jason bent down and felt George's neck for a pulse. He rolled George over, dark blood oozing from his mouth, his eyes lifeless. His shirt was drenched in blood. Below him lay the thin lifeless body of Scott saturated in blood. Jason fell to his knees.

"Scott," Jason cried his name tugging his shoulder. Scott moved. He coughed and crawled from under George's body with Jason's help. "Are you hurt?"

Scott shook his head from side to side and looked down at George and back at Jason. The tears cascading down his friends face told him what he dreaded.

A waiter from the restaurant approached. "Are you boys hurt?" He stopped and winced, almost taking a step back when he noticed the blood weeping from George's body. "We've called for the police and an ambulance."

Jason looked up through tear-saturated eyes. A crowd started to gather around. Scott threw up mostly on himself and started to sob.

"He saved me. He threw himself on me." Scott cried and threw up again.

"Is that your dad, sonny?" the waiter asked.

"No it's—" Jason stopped himself. He looked at the gathering crowd. A lady bent down and felt George's pulse. Jason thought she must be a nurse; she seemed to know what she was doing.

"He's gone boys. Is he your father? Where's your mother?" she asked Jason. Scott threw up again and didn't seem to mind his vomit and snot hanging from his nose and mouth. He shook violently, clearly shaken by the experience.

Jason pulled Scott up onto his feet. Scott sobbed and hugged him, his vomit rubbing on the side of Jason's face.

"Can I clean him up in the restroom please?" Jason asked the waiter.

"Sure son, go on through," the waiter replied.

Jason took Scott's hand and led him into the restaurant. Everyone's eyes followed the two boys. Inside, he made his way to the back, following the signs to the emergency exit. He went out the back way and closed the door behind them.

He stopped and cupped Scott's face in his hands and focused on his friend's eyes. "Scott we can't hang around here. We have to get back to the barracks. Are you sure you're not hurt?"

Scott said nothing. His large brown eyes looked through his friend, not focusing on anything in particular. He wiped his mouth and nose on the sleeve of his coat. It was blood soaked and made it worse. Jason took Scott's coat off, discarded it, and gave him his own. He took Scott's hand and pulled him, slowly jogging away from the back of the restaurant.

By the time they made it to the corner, they could here sirens from what Jason guessed would be either an ambulance or the police. The journey was around two miles. Jason pulled Scott along and took him down the embankment. Jason knew it came out near a playing field and across the street would be the barracks.

Scott pulled back. He was crying, exhausted, his body still shaking uncontrollably.

"Scott," Jason gasped. "We're almost there, come on mate," he put his arm around Scott to help him. "We can walk if you're tired once we get to the barracks. We will get SYUI to help us."

"He saved my life, and we just left him lying in the street surrounded by strangers," Scott said.

Jason sighed. "We can't do anything for him. They think you're his kid. It's not safe out here for you, and I don't know what to do. Let's get back to safety and go from there." Jason noticed Scott was looking over his shoulder. He turned to see what Scott was looking at.

"Oh no." Jason cursed.

"Well look who we have here," a man's voice said. It was the same group of men Jason had earlier escaped from, the Creggen Cleaners.

"Leave us alone." Jason cursed. "I'm not in the mood for you. I have to get my friend home."

The four men ran towards them. Jason almost threw Scott behind him and concentrated. Scott fell to his knees and seemed unsure what to do. He couldn't fight a kid his own size let alone an adult. Jason forced adrenaline into his system. He raised himself onto his toes and stood in a fight stance.

The first man raised his hand to hit Jason. It was a foolish move. Jason caught his hand and twisted it. He swung on it and used it as a pendulum. He swung and kicked the man's legs away from him. As the man was falling, a second approached and punched Jason. He blocked it, but the momentum sent him down on the ground. He rolled over and jumped up on his feet.

One man looked about forty with a large belly caught Scott by the collar and smacked him across the face. Jason witnessed it from the corner of his eye. He watched his friend get knocked to the ground.

Jason's eyes darkened. He was incensed and seem to step outside himself. Only a few times had he lost his temper this severely. An inferno ignited in his head. He threw himself at the man who hit Scott. In a single move Jason caught the man's collar with his left hand pulled his victim towards him and ducked a swing. He imagined he had hold of a tennis ball to increase his fist size and threw his right fist. The crack of the man's nose could be heard from across the street.

Jason span on his left leg, his right leg fired from his body and smashing into the wounded man's windpipe, sending him back several feet before he collapsed.

A baseball bat cracked across Jason's right shoulder. Ignoring the pain, he caught the bat, jerked it away from his attacker, and brought it down on the man's skull. He swiftly span around and used it to block another attack. Jason dived to the ground, rolled, and swung the bat across the face of his attacker. Scott cringed when he heard the crack as it smashed into the man's face. Blood spattered from his nose and mouth. His eyes closed and he made a gurgling sound, flailing his arms feebly as he fell backwards.

Jason could smell the blood, almost

welcoming the next man as he was charged. Jason switched back to his karate stance, took a step forward, and chambered both his hands, palms forward, elbows bent, the right at shoulder height the left at waist height. "Kia," Jason shouted in warrior style and launched a double palm strike focusing through the man's body. Both strikes landed on prime acupuncture points. But rather than heal and relieve pressure, the savage blows sent Jason's victim into spasm. To finish him off, Jason span on his right leg and threw a roundhouse kick.

The last man, who Jason suspected was the leader, pulled a sawn-off shotgun from under his jacket. Before he could take aim, Jason dived at the armed man's feet, swung his legs up, and kicked the gun up into the air. He threw a kick to the man's stomach, knocking him back several feet. Jason caught the shotgun as it was coming back down, pointed it, and walked forward towards the man. His eyes black as death itself and gritting his teeth, Jason aimed.

The entire fight had taken less than thirty seconds. All four men lay on the ground. Above one man stood one of the scariest sights Scott had ever seen. Jason Steed panting and aiming the gun at the man who looked petrified.

"Jason no," Scott shouted. He got up and ran towards them. Jason was motionless, his body trembling. "No Jason." Scott pulled his shoulder.

Jason swung around and caught Scott by his throat. His left thumb bedded deep into his friend's windpipe. His right hand still pointed the shot gun at the man who was on his back with hands raised, trying to squirm away. It was then when Scott noticed his eyes. It terrified Scott. The look was something no one could describe. George had once told him he had seen Jason '*loose it,*' as he put it, a few times, and he was pleased he was never on the receiving end.

Scott tried to pull Jason's hand away from his throat. "It's me Jason," Scott choked. Jason blinked and looked at his friend and nodded. He released his grip.

"Are you okay? Did they hurt you?" Scott asked, rubbing his throat. Jason threw the shotgun across the field. The man rolled over got to his feet and ran off.

"Um maybe, I thought they hit you," Jason said rubbing his shoulder. "Come on, we better move." Jason put his arm around Scott. Sweat and specks of blood covered his face. He was exhausted. Scott felt him getting heavy. They walked halfway across the playing field, and Jason stumbled, falling to his knees. Scott bent down.

"Are you all right mate. Are you hurt?"

Scott asked.

Jason wiped the sweat from his face. "That's one thing about pain." Jason groaned, rubbing his shoulder. "It commands to be felt."

"Can you walk?" Scott asked, helping him to his feet. He stood in front of Jason, still holding him.

"I'm exhausted and light headed."

"So that's the famous adrenaline rush you force into your system," Scott said, taking a pack of mints from his pocket. He pushed three into Jason's mouth. "Chew these. You burnt your sugar levels. This will help." Scott paused, looking at his friend. "You sure you are okay? You went a bit crazy back there."

"I thought they hurt you when he hit you. I just went. Well, no one hits you Scott," Jason said, crunching the mints.

Scott hugged Jason. "I love you mate." For a few seconds, Jason did nothing until it felt awkward.

"Agh you're squeezing my shoulder." Jason groaned and pulled away. "That guy caught my shoulder with the bat. All the karate training I do can never take pain like this away."

"I guessed as much. But you did take down four guys armed with baseball bats and a shot gun," Scott said.

Jason looked at his friend and smiled. If anything, at least the attack brought Scott back to his senses and out of shock. Together, they walked to the army barracks.

CHAPTER NINE

The army had left Scott and George alone and were not given any details of the mission. When Scott came back covered in blood with Jason, they offered help but no questions were asked. Scott called Paddy Murphy; he came back to the barracks. Not very many people were in the loop on the undercover operation for Jason's protection. Scott had no one else to call.

An army doctor cleaned Jason's cut hands and a cut just above his eye. Jason followed him into Scott's dorm room. It would normally sleep twenty soldiers; Scott had it to himself.

After a shower, Scott climbed into his bed, still shaking. Jason sat on Scott's bed and felt his friend's forehead. "You don't feel cold. I think you're in shock."

"I've never seen a dead person before," Scott said bluntly.

"I know, it's not nice. I've seen too many, but I never wanted to see someone I liked. I'm really gonna miss George," Jason croaked, fighting back tears.

"You can only like someone so much… But never like them as much as you are gonna miss them," Scott said. Jason looked at Scott, trying to decipher what he had just said. A knock at the door brought him back to his senses.

Paddy Murphy stepped in and paced towards the two boys. "What terrible news, are you boy's hurt in anyway?" he asked.

"Scott's badly shaken up. I have a few cuts and bruises and my shoulder is killing me, but I'm fine. Has someone informed Jean and Martin?" Jason said.

"Jean? Martin?" Paddy asked.

"George Young's wife and son."

"I believe that's happening right now. The Prime minister has been informed of course. MI6, MI5, and most of SYUI have been informed. Many will miss George, but SYUI must go on. For now, they're appointing a temporary replacement. She is on her way here now. She wanted to personally investigate this mission. Her reputation precedes her. She is tough and has been known to make grown men cry just by barking orders at them. She plays it all by the book; she won't bend any rules," Paddy said.

"*She*?" Jason asked.

"Yes, a career minded woman called Brenda Hatchet."

"It will be strange working with someone who doesn't curse, stink of body odor and cigarettes, farts, burps, and bends the rules a little." Jason paused, his eyes welled up. "Okay, bends the rules a lot." He tried to smile. His emotion brewing over, he sobbed. Scott took his hand and gently squeezed it.

"Is the mission over?" Scott asked.

Paddy looked at the two boys and shrugged his shoulders. "I suspect so. We will let Brenda decide. They are flying her here from London. Why don't you boys get some sleep? Jason do you want me to get someone to bring in a bed for you?"

Jason shook his head no. He lay down on top of the blankets next to Scott.

"I'll leave you guys alone to get some sleep. You both look wrecked."

*

Brenda Hatchet was flown in to Belfast from London by Helicopter. She arrived three hours later and was debriefed by Paddy Murphy. After going through the files and catching up on the details, she marched into the barrack room Scott used. Paddy followed behind like a terrified mouse.

Both boys were asleep. Scott was covered under the blankets and Jason lie on top of the bed, snuggled beside him.

"Look at them, it's disgusting," Brenda turned and said to Paddy. "Using boys this age. They're just children."

"I agree. If you could have seen them earlier crying over George, it was pitiful. But Jason here, he's the blond one," Paddy pointed, "he's one of SYUI's most successful secret agents. No one ever suspects him, but apparently he can take care of himself. Me, I'm like you and think they should be at school and should leave this stuff to grown-ups," Paddy said.

"Looking at the bruising and cuts to his hands and face, it doesn't look like he can take care of himself that well." She paced towards them.

"Wake up I need to speak to you," She shouted.

"I guess you don't have children yourself, do you?" Paddy grinned. He approached Jason and gently shook his arm. Jason opened his eyes and propped himself up on his elbow. He wiped his eyes and yawned.

"Did anyone see you when George was

shot?" Brenda asked.

"What?" Jason asked he sat up.

"The report said you were at the scene. Did anyone recognize you and see you?" she asked impatiently. Scott opened his eyes.

"Who?" Scott asked with one eye open.

"Go back to sleep mate," Jason said he climbed to his feet and faced Brenda.

"Let's take this conversation over there. He's tired and still shaken up," Jason said, gesturing to a table in the corner with his head.

"I need to talk to him as well." Brenda stiffened.

"And you will tomorrow. Now who are you?" Jason asked.

Brenda studied the boy. He was just as his file said he would be: disobedient and strong-minded. "I'm Brenda Hatchet the new head of SYUI."

"Acting head," Paddy interrupted and was immediately given a dirty look for his comment.

Jason shook her hand. "Hi. What do you

need to know?"

"When the gunman shot George did, anyone see you who might know you?" Brenda asked.

"It was Shamus O'Neill who shot and killed George Young. He never saw me. Some people from the restaurant did, but none know me."

Brenda shuffled through her papers and read a section. "It says here the gunman was hooded. So how can you be sure it was Shamus?"

"The way he walked, stood, his clothing, build, it was Shamus."

"But you are not one hundred percent sure?" Brenda quizzed.

"Ninety percent."

Brenda paused again, shuffling the notes and sucking on a pen. She questioned Jason for another hour before stopping and going over her notes. Jason fought off sleep. He looked at Paddy and tapped his wrist, the universal language for what time is it?

"It's nearly four in the morning son," Paddy said.

Brenda looked over her glasses at Paddy and frowned at him. Jason observed her. No wedding ring, probably aged around thirty, very slim. She spoke with an upper class English accent. Her hair was straight and long; nothing was out of place.

Brenda faced Jason. "Let me make myself clear from the start. Boys your age should be playing with train sets and going camping with the Boy Scouts. You shouldn't be running around the streets of Belfast getting shot at and definitely not working undercover as a spy. *If* I'm promoted head of SYUI permanently, this will be your last mission until you are least twenty-one and only if you qualify." She paused, looked over at Scott who was still asleep, and continued.

"However, we're here now and we have some new intelligence so against my better judgment, we need you to go back in."

"Is your cover blown, laddie?" Paddy asked.

"Um, no I don't think so. They probably think I'm in bed. If I can get back, they won't know I was gone."

"Do you normally travel around with blood and vomit on your clothes? And with cuts and bruises on your face?" Brenda smugly asked.

Jason looked down at himself. "Scott threw up all over himself and was squashed by George when he was shot. He was upset and needed a hug. I'll shower and borrow some of Scott's clothes. We're the same size."

"And how will you explain the new clothing to the O'Neill's?" Paddy asked.

"I'll say they're Gober's."

"Gober?" Brenda asked.

"Gobnait O'Grady. He's a friend," Jason said, talking off his clothing he paused. "What new information do you have?"

Brenda stood and walked over to him. "We ran the initials you gave us, *SS,* through our systems. We have heard those initials a few times lately. We have certain peoples phone lines tapped and…" she paused and gasped as Jason removed his shirt. "Oh Jason, what happened to your shoulder?" Brenda said before Jason interrupted her and pointed at her. Using his finger in a circular motion, he asked her to turn around while he continued to get undressed.

"A guy with a baseball bat hit me. It's just bruised but bloody hurts." Jason grimaced, removing the last of his blood and vomit-covered clothing.

Brenda faced away and continued. "It seems this person is the main arms supplier. We have never been so close, and he's coming to Belfast. We need you to…" Brenda paused again. The shower started to run. She waited for him.

The shower felt warm and refreshing. He was happy to get clean again and even happier when he raided Scotts suitcase of clothing. It was better than the clothing he had been forced to wear.

"I'm decent. You can turn around again," Jason said pulling on his shoes.

"Well, as I was saying, we need you to find out when he's coming. Anything you pick up could be vital to saving countless lives and many people from injury," Brenda said.

"We have a few problems I never mentioned. Scott was seen by Shamus. They assume he's George's son so he will need a baseball cap and change of clothes and maybe glasses to disguise him before he meets me to pass information. Also Um…" He paused, looking guilty. "Have you heard of the Creggan Cleaners?"

Brenda shook her head, saying no.

Aye, I have. A bunch of vicious vigilantes.

It's believed they run in the same circles as the IRA. Why, what have you done?" Paddy asked.

"They got too nosey for their own good and then one of them hit Scott," Jason said.

"Oh boy." Paddy sighed and sat down heavily, shaking his head.

Brenda looked bewildered. "What's the big issue with hitting Scott?" Brenda asked.

Paddy shook his head. "How bad did you hurt them Jason?"

"It was a mess. There was four of them armed with baseball bats and a sawn off shot gun. It wasn't going to be easy in normal circumstances, but when they hit Scott I kind of…" He paused.

"I've read your file and read Georges notes about your temper. You lost control?" Brenda asked.

Jason nodded. "None of them are dead." He gave a tight-lipped smile. "So maybe it's not so bad. Oh, and the good news is, I found out who is head of the IRA and gives the orders to Shamus."

"Who?" Paddy and Brenda said in

harmony.

"Bradan O'Neill."

"You're as nutty as a fruitcake, laddie. Bradan O'Neill is a retard, everyone knows that. I knew it was pointless sending in a boy to do a man's job," Paddy said aggressively.

"You're the retard, Paddy." Jason cursed at the top of his voice. It woke Scott up.

"You stupid little boy. Bradan is no more head of the IRA than I'm Cinderella," Paddy taunted.

"I dunno you look like one of the ugly sisters and have the brains of a pumpkin," Jason snapped.

Brenda got between the two of them and stopped them from throwing insults at each other before it got out of hand. Paddy was told to wait outside. With a blanket wrapped around himself, Scott joined Jason and Brenda. Jason passed him a folded piece of paper.

"This is one of Bradan's drawings, looks like animals or something," Jason said.

"It's a map." Scott said instantly and showed them the various markings. He soon deciphered Bradan's drawings and the location.

"How could you work that out so quickly?" Jason asked.

"I was just born awesome," Scott said as a matter of fact.

*

Paddy drove Jason and Brenda to Shankill Road where Jason was dropped off. He jogged the rest of the way, just to be safe in case someone was watching.

The milkman was already out on his round picking up empties and delivering fresh milk on the doorsteps. Jason gingerly opened the front door and crept in the house. The familiar stench of stale cigarettes welcomed him. He took off his shoes and tip toed up the stairs, staying close to the edges as it was less likely to squeak.

"And where the bloody hell have you been?" Bradan asked.

He made Jason jump. "Um. I was with Gober. I never knew it was so late, sorry," Jason said.

"Oh you will be when Maude sees you." Bradan grinned as he noticed Maude coming from her room, tying the cord around her dressing gown.

"Jason Norris what time do you call this?" Maude shouted she paced toward Jason. "Sneaking off into the night and what happened to your face. Have you been fighting again?"

Jason paused, thinking about his excuse. "Sorry Maude, I arranged to meet Gober. We went out and lost track of time and some boy's started on us. We fought them off then some others came and we had to hide."

"And exactly what was so engaging that kept you boys out until five in the morning?" Shamus barked, coming out onto the landing wearing his pajamas. Jason was repulsed by Shamus. His bitterness towards him turned to anger. He fought to control himself.

"When we were out, some poor man got gunned down in cold blood in front of his son downtown. The place was alive with police and the army. We just played ducking down and not being seen by anyone." Jason couldn't hide the contempt he felt for Shamus in his voice.

"Did anyone see you?" Bradan asked.

"No, it was just a game we played, like hide and seek. Sorry for being out so late. We couldn't just walk home because the police were everywhere. I don't know if they caught the *cowards* that shot the poor *unarmed* guy who was out for dinner with his kid. Isn't that terrible Shamus? Suppose that was us." Jason said, waiting for his reaction.

Bradan and Shamus said nothing. Maude looked guilty. "I will be glad when all this is over. Jason's right. What about the poor kiddie who watched his daddy get shot? Now Jason, to bed with ya, and where did these clothes come from?" Maude asked.

"I fell in the creek, so Gober let me borrow these. Goodnight Maude, and I'm sorry for sneaking out."

"So you should be. Don't think you got away with it either. There will be no playing with that Gobnait for two weeks. He's a bad influence on you. Now get to bed, we've church in the morning," Maude said.

CHAPTER TEN

Maude went into Jason's bedroom. He was in a deep sleep, curled up under his covers. She gently shook Jason. "Come on, Jason. It's time to get up. We have church today."

Jason felt like he had only just gone to bed a few minutes before. Had the previous night been a bad dream? Maude pulled the covers off him.

"Come on up, you jump and don't be forgetting to brush your teeth."

Jason swung his legs over the side of the bed. He rose, shivering in the cold air, and went to the bathroom before plodding barefoot downstairs in his pajamas. A mug of steaming hot tea welcomed him. He sat down opposite Bradan whose head was buried in the Belfast Daily Times. Jason wrapped his hands around his mug of tea and savored the warmth.

"Here's your toast. If you want jam, help yourself," Maude said.

"Thank you," Jason said quietly.

Shamus looked over the top of his paper. "You got a big bruise on your face, Jason. That must have hurt." He looked at Jason spreading jam on his toast. "But looks like you put up a good fight. You don't have a single knuckle that's not cut."

"Don't encourage him, Shamus. I don't want him fighting and coming back in that state. What will Jerry Duffy say if he sees the boy all cut up like that?"

Jason kept his head down and ate his breakfast. He was tired and knew it would be a long day.

*

Father Doherty gave his sermon mostly on the evils of alcohol and gambling. Jason was certain, if it was not for the hard wooden pew he sat on, he would have fallen asleep. Father Doherty was a gangly man with a raw face, partly paralyzed on one side. His affliction made him look as if he was trying to be funny, even when he wasn't.

The choirboys looked just as bored as Jason. A few glanced at him. His cheek was badly bruised right up to his eye. Father Doherty asked the choir to stand and announced they would sing a song to remind us of our love ones present and past.

It immediately struck a chord with Jason.

He thought of George Young. The choir started singing Ave Maria, some parts as a group and one part a choirboy sang a solo. Jason lowered his head, his thoughts with George and the times he had spent with him. The velvet angelic voice singing the high notes caused Jason to brim over with emotion.

Tears dropped around Jason's feet. His nose ran, which he wiped with the back of his hand. It was all he could do to control his emotions. When the hymn was over, he welcomed Father Doherty asking the congregation to kneel to pray. It gave Jason a chance to wipe his eyes.

When Shamus, Maude, and Jason were leaving the church, Father Doherty shook their hands and thanked them for coming.

"It's nice to meet you, Jason. Maude told me all about you. That's a nasty bruise you have there," Father Doherty said, pointing at Jason's face.

"Yes he was up to mischief and will pay for it," Maude said.

"Only God can judge us if we misbehave," Father Doherty preached.

"Really? Then Santa has some explaining

to do," Jason said.

Father Doherty gave Jason a disapproving look but never came up with a reply. As they headed down the church path, Shamus noticed someone.

"Maude would you look at the state of Delaney? Looks like he's been in a car accident or been hit by a bus," Shamus said, striding towards him. Maude and Jason followed.

"Delaney what in God's name happened to you? You look like you've been thrown over a cliff and dragged back up again by your face," Shamus barked. The man Shamus called Delaney looked up. Jason was on the opposite side of Maude. He peered past her. His heart skipped a beat. It was one of the Creggan Cleaners he had fought the night before. He ducked back, trying to hide.

"Maude can I go home now? I'm tired," Jason said.

"That's your fault for being out half the night with Gobnait. Let me find out what happened to Delaney first," Maude said.

Jason watched as Shamus and Delaney shook hands. He kept his head down and tried to hide behind Maude. Delany had his arm in a sling.

His nose was bandaged, and he was walking with what looked like a painful limp.

"What happened?" Shamus asked.

"Shamus O'Neill, nice to see you and Maude." Delaney coughed and spat on the ground. "Don't ask. I'm trying to put it behind me," Delaney said.

"Well it looks like you had the stuffing beaten out of you. Were you on alone?" Shamus asked.

"No I was with..." He paused and looked around to make sure no one else was in earshot and looked back at Shamus. "With the others. We were just keeping the neighborhood safe, and well, let's just say, appearances can deceive you. What you think is a tiny mouse can have a bite bigger than a lion. That's all I can say about it."

"Ah well top of the morning to you." Shamus grinned. He watched Delaney limp away.

A large lady came out of the church. Shamus nudged Jason. "Just imagine," he said, jerking his thumb at the large lady, "being married to that!"

Jason spent most of Sunday afternoon catching up on his sleep and doing his homework for Monday. Occasionally, he came close to breaking down when he thought of George. Jason enjoyed most aspects of working undercover and knew there would be times when people he cared for would get hurt. That was something he would have to try and get used to. What was hard was keeping the act up in front of Shamus.

*

"Uh-oh, looks like you bumped into the Mcgintys?" Gobnait asked when he saw Jason at the school gate. He took a closer look. "Jeez, looks like you really got your head kicked in." He placed his hand on Jason's shoulder.

"Agh, don't Gober," Jason said, pulling away. "My shoulder is really bruised."

"Sorry, I guess the Kung Fu stuff didn't help this time?" Gober sniggered.

"I guess not." Jason shrugged.

"I heard you won your race at the pool and Shamus and Reverend Flanagan were seen shaking hands," Gobnait said, squeezing a zit on his chin.

"Yeah, I was swimming with Cailin, his daughter. The team lost, but we managed to win our race."

"Cailin Flanagan? I've seen her. Not bad looking for a Unionist."

"Gober, I went out Saturday night on my own. You know, like we did when I stayed at your place? I kinda got into a scuffle… Anyway, I told Maude and Shamus I was with you," Jason said sheepishly.

"Me? So if Maude sees my mom then I will get my ass whacked on a count of you lying," Gobnait said.

"Um, I'm sure that won't happen, but I'm grounded for two weeks and now she thinks you're a bad influence on me." Jason sniggered.

"Me? I was home in me bed and now I'm a bad influence and caused you to get beat up like that?" Gobnait walked ahead. Jason ran after him and pulled him back.

"Hey sorry Gober. I was in a pile of trouble. I was trying to dig myself out of a hole," Jason said, smiling at him while raising his eyebrows.

"Why are you smiling at me like that? Your pretty blue eyes won't help," Gobnait said.

"Look sorry. Please just tell this white lie for me if they ask? I'll owe you big time," Jason said. He was disappointed his smile didn't work. It always seem to work on his father, girls, or Scott.

"I'll think on it but if I get my butt whacked you will owe me ten favors," Gober said.

CHAPTER ELEVEN

Monday night was swimming night. As usual, when Jason walked up the steps to the pool, a mirror was positioned as the swimmers entered the pool area so they could make final adjustments to swim wear if they needed. He paused and studied his shoulder. It was severely bruised, a dark purple color.

"Jason, what happened to your face?" Cailin smiled, looking concerned. "Oh and your shoulder! Were you in a car accident?"

"Hi Cailin. No, I got into a fight with someone," he said.

"I'm guessing you lost. It's looks painful, is it?" she asked.

"I want to be brave and say nah, but yeah, my shoulder is agony if I touch it," Jason said.

"Then I suggest you don't touch it." Cailin laughed.

"Oh we have jokes! I noticed your mum dropped you off. Can I walk you home? Maybe get some hot chips on the way?" Jason asked.

"I'm supposed to walk back with Coach Gloria. She lives near us, but I can tell her mom came after all."

"Oh," Jason said embarrassed. "About the chips... I don't have any money."

Cailin smiled at him as they walked to join the rest of the group. She allowed the back of her hand to rub against his. Jason retaliated and applied a small amount of pressure. To anyone watching, they were just walking close. Cailin felt as if she was holding his hand.

They joined the rest of the swimming group and started swimming widths with the others under the strict instruction of the coach. Jason noticed Scott up in the spectator's balcony watching them. He later met Jason when the swimming session was over. Seeing Jason up close, his shoulder looked worse. The bruise was as dark as a ripe plum and spread down his arm.

"Oh that looks nasty. Does it hurt?" Scott asked as Jason came out the shower.

"*Noooooooooooo*. Of course it hurts. Are you some kind of Eejit?" Jason said, doing his best to sound Irish.

"What did you call me? E*ejit*? That *Battle Axe Brenda* wants to send me back to England. I don't like her she's so serious. For now I can stay, but not sure how much longer," Scott said.

"Battle Axe Brenda?" Jason laughed. "As soon as we can find out who this SS guy is and get out of here, I'll be happy. I can't stand being under the same roof as Shamus. Maude is nice. She cares about me."

"Maude is nice she cares about me is like saying Hitler liked puppies so he was nice. She knows what Shamus is doing, buying and planting bombs blowing up people, shooting George and anyone else they want. Yeah she sounds really nice," Scott said.

Jason stopped getting dressed and looked at him. "Yeah you're right. I forgot that bit. It's difficult living with the enemy. It's like living in a Wolf's Lair."

"Wolf's Lair? Sounds like you have been learning your history finally. That's what they called Hitler's secret bunker," Scott said.

"You're not the only one with a brain."

"I told Battle Axe Brenda I would probably walk back with you half way home tonight. She was concerned I wouldn't get back to the barracks safely and asked me to call if not."

"Call her. You can't walk with me. I'm walking Cailin home. That reminds me, have you got some money I need to buy chips? I hate having no money. How are you supposed to take a girl out if you are skint?"

"You want me to call Battle Axe Brenda and go back with her and give you *my* money so you can impress some girl you are walking with so you can cheat on Catherine? I thought we were close friends."

Jason wrung his wet shorts out and studied his friend. "Scott, you and I are best friends. I'm not cheating on Catherine. We are no longer going out. We drifted apart. We never see each other. We are just friends. I'm undercover, so I have to make friends here and make it real," Jason said. "I find it hard having no money."

"What if she wants to make out?" Scott asked. "What would you do then?"

"I hope she does. I really like her." Jason grinned.

"Jason Steed, you're an animal. Typical son of a navy man. You want to have a girl in every port. You're like a girl addict." Scott said. "I wonder if *girlaholic* is the correct word. If it's in the dictionary, I bet it says: Girlaholic, someone like Jason Steed."

"What's wrong with that?"

Scott thought for a moment and grinned. "Make sure they have a friend for me too then."

Cailin waited for Jason outside the entrance to the pool building. She dug her hands in her pockets, trying to keep warm. Jason kept her waiting while he was trying to get his hair just the way he liked it. The chlorine made it feel flat and greasy, even after a shower. He finally appeared and smiled at her. He thought she looked beautiful. She wore a red knitted hat to keep the cold night air off her wet hair. Jason studied her as he approached. Her breath sent out a delicate steam circle around her face that gave her an angelic saint like appearance.

"And they say girls take a long time to get ready. I'm freezing," Cailin said.

"They also say good things come to those who wait," Jason said, taking her backpack from her and throwing it over his right shoulder with his. His left hand took her right hand.

"So you think you're a *good thing*?" She led the way.

"Sure, but then I need to be, to hold hands with the best looking girl in Belfast."

Cailin concealed her smile. She held his hand firmly. Jason wasn't quite sure when it happened. Or how it started. All he knew for sure, was he was falling in love and he could only hope she was feeling the same as him. His fingers wrapped around her hand. They occasionally glanced at each other and could do nothing other than smile at each other.

"The fries at the fish shop are normally greasy. There's another one a bit further along," Cailin said. "Although what kind of boy asks you out for fries and then says he has no money?"

"I have money. I borrowed it from someone." Jason hoped Cailin would not ask who it was from. He didn't want to lie to her. He was enjoying the moment. Her hand felt small and soft in his.

"You didn't have to do that Jason. I know you're fostered. It's not your fault. My dad has more money than most. I can pay."

"I know, I've seen your home. Maybe I should be a vicar when I grow up. Looks like you get paid well."

"I can't see you wearing a dog collar. Besides, what religion would you be, Protestant or Catholic?"

"I was joking," Jason said, changing the subject.

They walked further and came to another fish and chip shop. Jason noticed how busy it was. He thought that others must have the same opinion as Cailin regarding the chips. He ordered a large serving of chips and two pickled onions. They walked out together, sharing the chips.

"I might not like pickled onions," Cailin said.

"Oh, I never thought. Well, I won't eat one either then."

"You could eat them both."

"No, because if I did we wouldn't be able to…" he trailed off.

"Wouldn't be able to what?"

Jason stopped and looked at her. "If I had onion breath I would be able to do this."

He moved closer to her, his face just inches away from her. They stood motionless. Jason looked deep into her eyes. He tore away her barriers and locked eyes. His nose two inches away, he slightly tilted his face and looked at her lips. She slightly turned her face at the opposite angle.

Jason moved closer, his lips just an inch

away from hers. She closed her eyes. Jason knew she was his. His warm lips connected to her, a small kiss followed by lips locking. Cailin was passive. Jason pressed harder against her lips. The chips and paper wrapping fell on the ground. He pulled her close to him. After a few seconds, he pulled back, tilted his head the other way, and kissed her again. After almost thirty seconds, they pulled back and smiled at each other and locked foreheads.

"I dropped the fries." Jason laughed.

"Was that ok?" Cailin asked. "Did you like it?"

Jason looked at her wide-eyed. He pulled his bangs away from his eyes. His eyes wide open, face glowing. "Yeah I really did. Did you?"

"I haven't really kissed a boy before, but I liked kissing you. I suspect you have kissed quite a few girls?" she said it like a question.

"No, well I have kissed *a* girl. I had a girlfriend once. Why do you think I have kissed a few girls? Was I that awesome at it?"

"Jason, you have good looks, blue eyes, blond hair, and you are the best male swimmer in our club for your age. All the girls talk about you."

Normally, Jason would color up after such a remark, but his cheeks were already glowing from the cold night air and excitement of making out with a girl he liked.

They walked back to Cailin's home holding hands. It was a twenty-minute walk, but it seemed to pass in seconds. They walked up the path the front door opened. Cailin's mother smiled at them.

"Hello Jason. Cailin where is Coach Gloria?" she asked.

Before she could answer Jason cut in so Cailin would not have to lie to her mother. "She had to help someone so I walked her home Mrs. Flanagan. I hope that was okay?"

She nodded. "Well you should have called, but you're home safe now. Say your goodbyes. Don't be all night; you both have school tomorrow."

Cailin gave her mother *the look*. There is no scientific explanation of *the look*. Every child aged ten and older has it and only his or her parents can understand the code. Basically, Cailin told her mother to get back in the house and leave her alone to say good night to Jason. Her mother quickly translated it and went back inside, leaving the door slightly a jar.

"Have we got to wait until next Monday to see each other again?" Cailin asked.

"I won't be able to get out on a school night, only Mondays for swim club. Maybe Saturday or Sunday?" Jason said.

"Sundays are out. I go to church all day, with morning service and other activities. Unless you want to come to church with me?"

"I don't think my foster parents would allow that. They take me to a Catholic church. It wouldn't go down well. Seems pointless to me. It's the same God and Jesus I bet most of the hymns they sing are the same."

Cailin leant back against the door frame. Jason put his hand over her shoulder on the frame and moved closer to her again. He was determine to kiss her again before he went home. Cailin submitted. The couple kissed again before Cailin broke it off. Jason pushed back and carried on kissing her.

Cailin responded for a few seconds and gently pushed him off again. "I can't meet you Saturday. Dad has a business meeting at the house with someone. I have to go to my grans with mum. The meeting is with this really important man. He comes to see dad about twice a year. Father is always nervous before he comes."

"Who's coming, the Pope?" Jason asked and kissed her again not, letting her answer. She grinned the kissed away, trying to speak while Jason continued to try and lock lips with her again.

"No, some English guy he calls SS," Cailin said before her lips were smothered again by Jason's.

Jason carried on kissing her and abruptly stopped and pulled back. "Did you say he was called SS?" His smile was gone. He was looking serious.

"Yes," Cailin said, expecting Jason to try and kiss her again. He noticed the disappointment in her face when he held back.

"Who is he?"

Cailin pushed herself off the doorframe and wiped her mouth with the back of her hand. "He's just a business associate of my father. Why, do you know him?"

"No, I've just heard the name before," Jason said. He stopped asking questions. Any more would look suspicious. Cailin's father came back to the door and opened it.

"Okay, go in now Cailin. It's getting late. And you better come with me, Jason. I will run you home in the car," Rev Flanagan said rattling his car keys.

"Can I come with you to take Jason home, Dad?" Cailin asked.

"No, you have spent enough time saying goodnight. Off to bed with you." Jason followed him down towards his car.

Rev Flanagan opened the driver's door and climbed in. He opened the front passenger door for Jason. Before Jason climbed in he threw a kiss to Cailin.

"So Jason, you like my Cailin it seems?" Rev Flanagan asked.

"Yes Sir, Reverend Flanagan."

"Well let's hope by the time you two are older all the troubles of Northern Ireland are behind us. Are you happy with your foster family, the O'Neill's?"

Jason grunted a short reply. His mind was spinning so fast he couldn't think straight. He wanted to know more about the person they call SS. Was it the same one that was working with the IRA and selling arms to Shamus and Braden?

If it was, why does he visit Rev Flanagan? And why are the meetings so important Cailin has to go out? Why is Rev Flanagan so wealthy? When can I see Cailin again? She was a much better kisser than Catherine. It was more grown up. Is she my girlfriend now? What happens after the mission is over? Am I in love with Cailin? He rested his forehead on the window and gazed out, not taking notice of the scenery.

Rev Flanagan stopped his car outside the O'Neill's home. Jason thanked him and climbed out. A few curtains twitched up and down the narrow street. Maude opened the front door. She wore curlers in her hair. She smiled at Jason and sneered at the driver of the car.

"Oh it's you. Well, thank you for running Jason home," she said to Rev Flanagan.

"Not at all, Mrs. O'Neill. He's a good lad. I'll never forget that race he won at the pool, and it seems Cailin likes him."

"Yes, well thank you for bringing him home."

He drove off and left Jason in a cloud of exhaust fumes.

CHAPTER TWELVE

Jason pulled on his pajamas and turned out the bedroom light. Gazing out the small bedroom window, his mind was elsewhere. How would he contact Scott or Battle Axe Brenda and inform them that the Rev Ian Flanagan is meeting SS on Saturday? Could it be the same person? As soon as he tried to put the pieces together, his mind went back to Cailin. Kissing her outside the fish and chip shop, not caring if anyone saw them.

"Am I in love Charlie Teddy?" Jason asked the stuffed toy. He climbed into bed and lay back, with his hands behind his head, staring up at the ceiling. If I am falling in love, it's like stepping into water, first slowly getting wet, then suddenly becoming completely submerged, and then I'm out of my depth. But it feels good.

Jason lay for hours. He didn't need to sleep and dream fantasies. His life was now better than any dream could ever hope to be.

The next two days passed like a sleepy haze. He found himself thinking of Cailin. They spoke on the phone after school but were only allowed ten minutes. Thursday night, Maude would be going to bingo. Jason hatched a plan to contact Scott and Battle Axe Brenda.

Gober couldn't help but notice Jason was head over heels with Cailin. She was all he spoke about. He agreed to help Jason call her on the schools nurse's phone. Although Jason had intentions of calling Scott, he went along with Gober's plan.

At lunchtime, when the lunch lady was not looking, Jason and Gober put some cut up carrots, mash potatoes, and some cake from their lunches in a plastic bag. Gober added some chocolate milk for good effect. Hiding under his jacket the boys left the canteen and made their way to the school library. They took cover behind a large shelf full of non-fiction books. After checking the coast was clear Gober took a mouthful of the mixture. He poured the rest on the floor.

Gober staggered out and made his way to the Liberian with Jason.

"Miss, Gober's not feeling well. He's just puked up all over the floor," Jason said.

Miss Pinkleton, the school Liberian, looked up over the top of her glasses and eyed Gober suspiciously.

"Uh-oh he doesn't look good," Jason said as Gober held his stomach.

Gober leant over and spat out the mixture on the Liberians desk. She jumped to her feet, trying to avoid his vomit.

"Really boy, did you have to do it on my desk?" she cried, trying not to vomit herself.

"Miss, shall I'll go and get the nurse?" Jason asked trying not to laugh. To his amazement Miss Pinkelton started to heave and threw up her elf in her wastebasket. "I'll take that as a yes then." Jason smirked.

Jason ran down the corridors. He came to the school nurses office and barged in.

"Miss, Gobnait O'Grady and Miss Pinkleton have both thrown up in the library. She asked me to get you," Jason said.

"Jason Norris you should knock before entering. What, both of them have been sick?" She frowned, picking up a bag and towel.

"Yes miss. I bet it was the school diner. The chicken looked half cooked to me."

She hurried down the corridor. Jason watched her large lumpy body bounce up and down while she hurried down a corridor. As soon as he watched her turn the corner, he went back in her office and picked up the phone and called the number George had previously given him.

To his annoyance it was not picked up until the fifth ring. "Hello," came an unfamiliar voice.

"This is Jason Steed I need to speak to Scott or Battle Axe urgently."

"Hello, Jason this is Paddy Murphy. Scott is not here, and who did you ask for?" Paddy asked.

"Battle Axe Brenda."

"Haha, you boys are so cruel. She's not here either."

"What's going on? That's Scott's job, to be there. I need to meet them tonight," Jason snapped.

"They should be back by tonight. They flew over to England to attend George Young's funeral."

"Oh, I never knew. I should have went but I'm stuck here."

"Jason, you are doing what George wanted. If you want to do something for George, keep working on the case and find out what you can. Tonight you say, where?"

"Have them meet me on the corner of Shankhill Road by the post office just after eight," Jason said.

"I will pass the message on Jason, stay safe young man," Paddy said.

Jason got out just in time before the school nurse got back with Gober. The plan worked much better than they had hoped for. Gober was sent home. While he waited for his mother to pick him up, Jason sat with him.

"Did you call your bird?" Gober whispered.

"Yeah thanks. Did you see Miss Pinkleton? She threw up for real. It was gross," Jason said, pulling a face as if he was going to be sick.

"I know, it was classic. She had diced carrots in her vomit too." He laughed.

*

A small, lonely figure tucked himself in the door way of the post office. He shuffled his feet and dug his hands into his pockets, trying to keep warm. How long had he been waiting? It must have been fifteen minutes. They were late. He looked up and down the street. An old man walking his dog and a few parked cars, other than that it was empty. Jason lifted his shoulders, almost trying to cover his neck and ears with them to keep warm.

Car lights gave away the location of a car travelling in his direction. Jason peered from his hiding place to get a better look. It slowed down to a crawl. He walked out onto the sidewalk and walked towards the car. It pulled over and an interior light came on. Jason noticed Paddy and Battle Axe in the front. Someone in the back opened the back door. Jason jumped in.

"You're late. It's bloody freezing standing there waiting for you," Jason said as the car pulled off.

"Hi Jase, we only just got back," Scott said.

"Hi Scott, you look smart. How was the funeral?" Jason asked, noticing Scott was wearing a black tie and blazer.

"It was a big deal. Four black horses and a carriage, over a hundred people following, a whole brigade of police turned out. His wife and son where there. It was sad," Scott explained.

"I even saw a few from the criminal underworld paying their respects. George may have been their enemy and even put a few in jail from time to time, but they still respected him," Brenda interrupted.

The tension between Scott and Paddy was picked up by Jason, who took his friends side and became off towards Paddy.

"Paddy said you have some urgent information?" Brenda asked.

"Yeah kinda strange really. Have you heard of the Reverend Ian Flanagan?" Jason asked.

"Of course we have. I may be Irish, but we are not all thick Jason," Paddy snapped.

"You said it." Jason shrugged.

Paddy stopped the car and turned and stared at Jason. "You've got a big mouth for a small boy."

Jason ignored him. "Like I was saying, Brenda, have you heard of him?"

Paddy spun the wheels of the car and pulled off again. Scott grinned at Jason and gave him a high five. Both boys seemed to take delight in annoying Paddy.

"Yes, he's a royalist and unionist. He's on our side against the IRA. He represents most protestant people who want to remain part of Britain."

Scott interrupted. "No, Brenda he's not on *our side*. George Young said we don't take sides. We are simply here to find out who is supplying the guns and bomb making equipment and report back. Then you arrest them, and we go home."

"Well you know what I mean," Brenda tutted.

"No we don't," Scott argued. "But anyway Jason, what of him?"

Jason took a deep breath and waited for everyone to calm down. "Well Rev Flanagan is meeting a business man on Saturday at his home. He meets him two or three times a year. This business man goes by the initials 'SS.' So if he's meeting him, and Shamus and Bradan also meet with him, this guy 'SS' must be selling arms to both sides."

"That's impossible. The Rev Flanagan is a man of the church. He's on our..." Brenda paused. "He's one of the good guys."

Paddy stopped the car on the side of the road and turned to Jason. "Is this information correct, boy?"

"No I just made it up for a laugh. Derrrr of course it's real, and if he is just a man of the church how come he lives in a great big house with new cars and the largest TV I've ever seen? It's ginormous. He's loaded," Jason said.

"Jason, who ever told you this is wrong," Paddy said. "He may have a large home, but he doesn't get paid that much." He shook his head from side to side. "What would the great George Young have said?"

"Well done."

He looked at Jason. "Or," added Paddy. "He might advise you not to be a silly little boy."

Jason's rage made him tremble. He pulled himself forward and starred at Paddy. "My information is correct. His house is huge. It's not just his TV; the whole place is like a palace inside. He wears a Rolex watch. His wife has one too, and his son has more records in his room than a Virgin music store. They have TVs in all the bedrooms as well. He's either taking money from the collection box, or he is dealing with this guy 'SS'.

"I doubt you've seen it with your own eyes. Rev Flanagan and Shamus are sworn enemies. No way would he let a brat of Shamus O'Neill's into his home," Paddy said.

"Are you calling me a brat as well as silly?" Jason frowned. "Brenda, what is the point of me giving you information if we have Paddy Murphy here doubting everything I say? I thought this was a SYUI mission. Why is he even here?" Jason cursed.

"Jason, Paddy is Irish Undercover intelligence. We are on the same side. He knows these people better than anyone," Brenda said.

"Well, tell Mr. Irish Undercover *un*-intelligence that Rev Flanagan invited this silly little brat into his home on more than one occasion, and I've seen it myself, and his daughter told me about Saturday."

The car went silent again. Jason sat back in the seat. Paddy eventually spoke.

"Sorry, Jason. You have done better than expected, and if you are correct and I am sure you are, then you have uncovered something that we didn't see. Well done. How did you get access into his home to see the bedrooms?"

"Cailin his daughter, she's thirteen and the

prettiest girl in Belfast. We swim in the same team, and I'm kind of, well her…" Jason paused.

"Her what?" Brenda asked.

Jason gave a nervous smile. "We are more than just friends."

"Jason Steed. I knew it! You stud. I bet you made out with her." Scott laughed, giving Jason another high five. Jason puckered his lips with a smile, closed his eyes, and nodded, looking rather pleased with himself.

"You're not here to start making out with girls, Jason," Brenda said.

"I know I'm undercover, but I had to play along. That's all I did at first. Then, I got carried away. Now I really, really like her, and she thinks the same about me. It just sort of snowballed into a girlfriend relationship. The good news is I found out about SS."

As Jason climbed out of the car, Paddy also climbed out of his seat and looked at Jason.

"I need to have a word with you," Paddy said, pointing his finger at Jason.

"You can have two words," Jason said callously. "Good-bye

CHAPTER THIRTEEN

A hundred feet from the Flanagan home, at a safe distance, sat a van painted with wording that read *Grady Gallagher's Plumbing, Number 1 Plumbers in the Number 2 Business.* Inside the back of the van were two SYUI agents armed with powerful binoculars and cameras with long distance lenses. The back windows were covered with a dark film, making it impossible to see in. They arrived just after nine in the morning and watched for any movement at the Flanagan home.

Just after ten, Cailin and her mother left the home together. They were going into Belfast city shopping. Cailins brother, Niall, had already left to play rugby with his friends.

For the next three hours, the SYUI team sat in the van and waited before something eventually broke the boredom.

A highly polished black Jaguar pulled up outside Rev Flanagan's home. A man in his sixties stepped out. He wore a white shirt, blue tie, and black pants. He opened the back door and pulled out his blazer. The SYUI team took picture after picture of him.

After pulling on his blazer, he checked his

grey handlebar moustache. He licked his thumb and forefinger and twilled each end. He collected a large case from the truck of his car, eyed up and down the street and marched, almost military style towards Rev Flanagan's home. The front door opened as he approached.

"Please come in, sir." Rev Flanagan smiled. The two men shook hands.

The old gent placed his case on the dining room table and, with two clicks, opened the case. Rev Flanagan peered inside at the explosives and smiled.

"Would you look at that, victory in a case. And here is something for you," Flanagan said. He passed the old gent a large bundle of cash. "It's a pleasure as always doing business with you, SS."

The man he called SS flicked the bundle of money in his hand. "Is it all here?"

"You know me better than that. Twenty thousand in cash and not a penny more. Daylight robbery, if you ask me, but we need to make an example of the IRA and let them know they don't own Northern Ireland," Flanagan said.

The old man stiffened and nodded. "Well, one must be off. When you need me again, the usual contact will work." He gave his hand to the reverend and Flanagan gave a quick shake. Then, he turned to leave. He took a few steps and froze in his tracks. He eyed a framed photograph on the mantel piece and snatched it, looking closing at the image. His face turned white, his eyes bulging wide in disbelief he gasped.

"That's my daughter Cailin. She had just won a race at her swimming club," Rev Flanagan said.

The old man held it firm with one hand and stomped his finger on the picture. "Bloody hell. It can't be. It just can't be. But boy does he look like him. Who's the boy with her?" He demanded.

"Oh that's her swimming partner, although I think they are sweethearts now." He paused and studied the panic stricken old man who was clearly agitated by the picture. "Do you know him?"

"What's his name?" SS asked.

"That's Jason, Jason Norris. He lives with a Catholic family. Not our sort of people, but she's young and she likes him. Great little swimmer he is, quite an athlete."

The man walked over to the couch. His

face had now turned ashen like he had seen a ghost. He slumped down, looking straight ahead. Rev Flanagan sat next to him and took the picture from him.

"Jason *Norris* you say?" SS asked.

"Yes, what of him? Do you know him?" Flanagan asked.

"*Norris*, well I never. I have to go." He never shook Flanagan's hand. He made his way to the front door and let himself out.

From outside, he looked up and down the street. His eyes narrowed as he focused on the van and sighed. He hurried down the steps to his car, jumped in, and pulled off. He stopped when he was level with the van and got out. He walked to the back of the van and opened the back door. Inside, two-startled SYUI officers faced him. Their cover was blown.

He pulled out a revolver and shot the two men point-blank before collecting the cameras and jumping back into his car. The Jaguar roared into life and sped off away from the scene.

*

SYUI and the police sealed off the area. Brenda Hatchet and Paddy arrived at the scene in

Paddy's Ford Cortina. They stepped out of the car and flashed their ID badges at the police and walked towards the van. The two bodies where still inside. A police photographer took pictures. Brenda strode towards the van and peered inside.

Brenda spoke to other SYUI officers and police. An ambulance was eventually allowed to take the bodies away. Later, the van was transported back to the army barracks. A forensic team went over it. Scott watched them working and read the notes they made.

The police went house to house asking questions. No one had seen anything. A few homes close said they heard gunshots and stayed well clear of the windows. Paddy Murphy had gone with the police to Rev Flanagan's home. Flanagan said he was writing a sermon for Sunday's service. He had been invited to a church in North Belfast. Paddy thanked him for his time and made his way back to the army barracks.

Brenda sat heavily in a chair. She was distraught. Losing two SYUI officers just a few days after she had taken over and on her orders would pay a toll on her. She looked up at Scott who was peering inside the van. Paddy returned and marched towards her. He looked at Scott who was looking inside the van and shook his head.

"What's wrong with that kid? Hasn't he seen enough blood? He should be at school, not here looking at that. It's not healthy, not bloody normal, for a kid to be staring at blood and brains scattered around the inside of van," Paddy said.

Scott heard him and stepped back from the van. He looked over the notes and paced up and down, trying to piece everything together.

"What did Flanagan have to say?" Brenda asked.

"Said he was writing a sermon. I don't believe him, and I have to admit it, Jason was right about Flanagan. He lives like a king," Paddy said.

"What did you say?" Scott asked.

"All right, don't rub it in. Your mate was right, and I was wrong."

"No, I'm not didn't mean that. I *knew* Jason would be right. What did you say about a king?" Scott asked.

"Oh, that Rev Flanagan lives like a king. His house has marble floors, the largest TV I have ever seen, and a Persian rug in front of the fire. The home is full of antiques, silver candlesticks, and oil paintings on the walls. And wouldn't you know it, just to rub it in, I see a picture of Jason smiling at me on the mantel, taunting me for being wrong," Paddy said.

"Jason's picture?" Brenda asked.

"Yes, with Flanagan's daughter in swim suits."

Scott went back to the van and watched the forensic team. He paced back fourth and looked at the notes over and over.

"What's his deal?" Paddy asked. He nodded in Scott's direction. Brenda stood and spoke quietly so Scott could not hear.

"I've read the notes. George Young was terrible with paperwork, but one thing he mentioned a few times and once in large letters underlined. Never doubt Scott again. I have not worked with these two boys before, and you know my feelings about having them even being here, but George Young was no fool. If he said not to doubt Scott Turner, then we have to let him do his thing. He has one of the highest IQ's in Britain. He may be a little nerdy, but that kid is smart."

"Smart ass if you ask me," Paddy said.

"Well I'm not asking, and like you said,

Jason was right earlier."

*

Jason offered to help Maude cook dinner. He didn't enjoy cooking, but it took his mind of what could be happening at Cailin's home when her father met the man she called SS. He was hoping the SYUI team would be able to get some pictures and follow him.

Maude passed a saucepan of potatoes to Jason. "Add two large dobs of butter and a splash of milk and smash them up while I check the sausages," she said.

He picked up the potato smasher and looked at her. "Two *dobs* of butter and how much is a dob?" He smiled.

"You can wipe that cheeky grin off your face young man." She dug a knife into the butter and scooped some out. "Here, this is a dob of butter."

The phone rang. Shamus and Braden were both on the couch watching football. Shamus sighed as he wearily hauled himself up and answered. Jason could hear the one-sided phone conversation.

"Hi, this is Shamus."

"What, right now?" Shamus said.

"Calm down. Yes, we can, but you told us Thursday. We don't have all the funds together yet," Shamus argued.

"Give it here," Bradan said, snatching the phone from his brother. "What the hell is the rush? You told our Shamus Thursday. What's the hurry?"

"Who do you think it is? It's Bradan," Bradan snapped when he was asked who he was.

Braden went quiet for a few moments before speaking again. "Okay, at the back of the park. It'll be me and Shamus. You'll have to accept what we have, and we will have to owe you the rest, but we can be there in fifteen minutes."

"You're not going out. We're having bangers and mash. Jason helped cook it," Maude complained.

"We'll have it later, Maude. Stick it in the oven. We have to meet someone," Shamus said.

"Must be important to come before your dinner," Maude snapped.

"It's SS," Shamus whispered. Jason

overheard and tension coiled around in the pit of his stomach in a tightly cinched knot. Shamus ran up the stairs. Bradan took the lid of the flour jar and dug his fingers into the white fluffy powder. He pulled out a plastic bag covered in flour and rinsed it off. Jason could just make out it was a bundle of money.

Jason pretended to ignore them and continued to smash the potatoes. Shamus came thundering down the stairs and back into the back room. He held something behind his back.

"Jason, we need to talk some business. Can you go to your room a few minutes, please son?" Shamus said.

"Yes, sir," Jason said. As he walked past Shamus, he could see the reflection of the back of Shamus on the TV screen. Shamus was holding two guns. Jason continued to his room and waited for them to leave. He planed to call SYUI and follow them.

*

Scott coughed to get Brenda's attention. She sat down and looked at him. Paddy looked on.

"I think I have worked out who this guy 'SS' is, and if I'm right, Jason could be in danger.

His cover is most certainly blown," Scott said.

"How the hell did you work that out?" Paddy said.

"*You* Paddy actually gave me the tip I needed. You said that *Flanagan lives like a king.* Jason once said the same thing but about another person. This was over a year ago. He mentioned back then that this guy *lives like a king*," Scott said.

"I'm lost Scott. So who do you think this guy is?" Paddy asked.

"First you have to raid Flanagan's home. SS sold him something, probably guns or bomb making equipment. If you go now, you could probably find what he just bought."

"Okay, but if you are wrong…" Brenda stopped herself. "Never doubt Scott," she said under her breath before continuing. "Consider it done. Who is SS?"

"We need to go back almost fourteen years. The IRA bomb that killed Jason's grandparents, it was before Jason and I were born. I've been reading the files because George thought Shamus was too blame. The file says that Mr. & Mrs. Steed had been to the theatre and they had been mistaken for a member of parliament and his wife. They had the same car, a black Rover." Scott paused before continuing. He started to pace up and down and waved his hands about as if he was conducting an orchestra while he spoke.

"So everyone thinks Raymond Steed's parents, Jason's grandparents were killed because of a case of mistaken identity," Scott said.

"Yes, that's correct. I read the file too. They had the same car," Brenda said.

"No, they didn't have the same car. Jason's grandfather had a black Rover P4. According to the statements, it was in the repair shop having work done on it. So Mr. Steed borrowed his brother's car, a newer Rover P5. *That* car was identical." Scott came to a stop and smiled. He looked disappointed when both Paddy and Brenda had blank faces.

"I think the IRA got the right car, it just had the wrong Mr. Steed in it. The IRA was after Mr. Steed's brother, the man Jason and his father call Uncle Stuart. Stuart Steed, his initials are SS. When Stuart Steed arrived at Flanagan's home today to sell either weapons or explosives, he must have noticed the picture of Jason. And after seeing the news regarding George Young, Stuart Steed must have worked out Jason was here working undercover."

"He went outside, and his suspicions where grounded when he noticed a van parked across the street with blacked out windows. He shot them and took the cameras because he knew he would be recognized." Scott stopped and took a drink of water.

"This is guess work?" Paddy argued.

"Remember, you said *he lives like a king?* Well I remembered who Jason said that about a year ago, it was his uncle, Stewart. He is a retired army colonel, but has a very large home and drives around in a new Jaguar. He is loaded. No wonder, if he is supplying arms to all the different paramilitary groups in Northern Ireland."

"Would he hurt Jason?" Brenda asked.

"No, he loves Jason. Last Christmas, he bought Jason a new bike, leather jacket, and gave him money. He does the same for Jason's dad. He gave him the latest Omega divers watch. He's always buying Jason stuff and pays for his school fees at St. Joseph's. How can he afford that type of thing on an Army Pension? He will have plenty of old army contacts," Scott said.

"If you're right Scott, those same arms are used on our own troops. That's sick." Paddy cursed.

"Let's go and raid Flanagan's home. If Scott's right, whatever he purchased will still be hidden in the home. Scott, stay here," Brenda said.

Within minutes, Brenda and Paddy left with an armed SYUI team and met up with police outside the Flanagan home. Four police cars, some with sniffer dogs, arrived.

*

Jason returned back to the living room. Maude served up two plates of sausages and mash potatoes, with onion gravy.

"Come on, Jason, all the more for us. You can't beat bangers and mash," Maude said.

Jason smiled at her. His eyes glanced to the telephone and darted over to the mantel clock.

"I have to see Gobnait," he said.

"That boy is trouble. You can see him Monday at school," Maude said.

Jason thought for a second. "I have a homework assignment and he's my science partner. We have done the work, but he has the results. I will run over to his place and pick it up before it gets dark." He turned and headed for the door.

"Jason Norris, you get back here now. I'll go with you after dinner," Maude called after him. Jason ignored her. He continued and slammed the door shut behind him. He ran down the street towards the park.

As he turned the corner, he stopped at the phone box. A large lady was using it. He noticed she had a pile of two pence coins next to the receiver. He knew that meant she was going to be talking for a while. He opened the door.

"Get out, I'm on the phone." Her voice had an edge of hysteria. She was in her fifties with a round face and tiny eyes that seemed too close together. She had odd colored curlers in her hair under a hair net.

"My mother fell down the stairs. I need to call an ambulance," Jason said.

She repeated the message to the person on the other end of the line and said she would call back. She placed the phone back on the hook, disconnecting the call.

"Do you want me to call?" she asked.

"No, please let me do it," Jason said,

moving between her and the phone. He dialed a number SYUI had given. He would not need money for the call.

The phone rang the other end and was eventually picked up. "Hello," a voice answered.

"This is Jason Steed. I need to speak to Brenda Hatchet or Paddy Murphy. It's urgent."

"Hello, Jason. I'm sorry they left. Scott is here," the man said.

"Put him on please," Jason said.

The woman opened the door to the phone booth. "Did you get through okay sonny?" she asked.

"Yes, I'm doing fine," Jason snapped, pushing her back out.

"Jason?" Scott asked.

"Scott! Shamus and Bradan are meeting SS now at the back of the park. Where's Battle Axe and Paddy?" Jason asked.

"They are in the middle of raiding the Flanagan's home," Scott said.

Jason paused. He thought about Cailin

and hoped she was not there while the home was being raided by SYUI. "Um. Is anyone useful there?"

"Thanks, I'll go back to being useless," Scott said.

"No, I didn't mean it like that. We need to catch this SS guy and catch Shamus and Bradan buying arms. I can't do it alone. Shamus and Bradan are armed," Jason said.

"Jason, there's something you need to know about SS, but it's kinda hard to tell you," Scott said.

"Scott, I have to go. Contact Battle Axe or gather up any of the SYUI team and get to the park."

"Okay, the SYUI forensic team is here. I'll get some of them and radio Battle Axe. But Jason, you really shouldn't go yourself. I need to tell you something about SS," Scott said.

"It doesn't sound like you are calling an ambulance. If you lied to me..." the woman shouted at Jason. She opened the door and forced her way in.

"Scott, I got to go." Jason dropped the phone.

"Scott? Who is Scott? You lied to me. You cried wolf, you horrible little brat, and I was talking to my daughter who is eight months pregnant." The woman spat. Jason darted out the phone booth and ran towards the park.

*

Just as Rev Flanagan was protesting for the fourth time regarding the raid and invasion of his privacy, SYUI found a box full of Gelignite in the closet hidden under the stairs.

"I haven't seen that before. You must have planted it," he said accusingly to Brenda, Paddy, and three SYUI agents.

"We know you met a known arms dealer today. If we find one fingerprint of yours on this box, you will be spending the rest of your life in prison," Brenda said. "Take him." Flanagan was arrested and handcuffed.

*

The main section of the park had a play area that included swings, a slide, and climbing frame. A mother pushed a toddler in a swing. A group of boys where kicking a football around on the large green. Jason noticed a couple of people walking dogs and a girl aged around nine and her father trying to get a kite up in the sky. He sprinted across the field through the football game to the wooded area at the back of the park. He was hoping it was not too late and he could catch SS and find out who he was.

CHAPTER FOURTEEN

A black Jaguar was parked on the edge of the park. The radio played brass military band tunes. Stuart Steed licked his thumb and forefinger and twirled his moustache. He used his drivers mirror to get the handlebar shape he preferred. In front of him, two men walked towards his car. Stuart climbed out and walked to the front of his car. He paused, took out his white handkerchief, and polished the chrome Jaguar that pounced from the hood of his car.

"SS, this is unlike you to change your plans. Should we be concerned?" Bradan said. Both Bradan and Shamus faced him but left a twenty-foot gap between them.

"Nothing that will concern you. One has

more business to attend to," Stuart said in his upper class British accent. He walked back to the trunk of his car and opened it. After checking the coast was clear he pulled out a black leather sports bag. He noticed a movement behind a shrub. He looked again and it was gone. Whatever it was, it stayed hidden. He nodded and smiled to himself before walking back to the front of his car.

"You have the money?" he stiffened.

"I have what we had at such short notice. The rest won't be available until next week," Bradan said.

Stuart Steed walked forward a few paces and gently dropped the bag on the grass. Shamus met him and passed him a brown paper bag full of cash before picking up the bag. Both men walked back to their previous positions slowly, each one not losing eye contact with the other.

"It appears you got sloppy Bradan. You and Shamus have been infiltrated," Stuart Steed said.

"What are you talking about man? We have not. Our cover is safe and secure," Shamus argued.

"You really are quite dumb. You were

even followed here and as we speak we are being watched," Stuart said.

Bradan and Shamus quickly looked around, not wanting to take their eyes off Stuart Steed and could see nothing. This area of the park was deserted apart from a few trees and shrubs.

"You're getting old and paranoid. We're alone," Bradan said.

Stuart Steed smiled and shook his head from side to side. "Okay Jason, you can come out now." Bradan and Shamus looked around. From behind a blackberry bush, Jason stood up.

"What the hell are you doing here, laddie? *Get* home," Shamus barked and looked at Stuart, his eyes almost popping out of his head. He looked back at Stuart Steed. "How'd ya know his name?"

Jason stepped closer, his sapphire blue eyes opened wide, looking at his uncle in disbelief.

"Uncle Stuart? What are you doing here? What are..." Jason said. He paused, his mind trying to piece everything together.

"*Uncle* Stuart?" Shamus asked. He looked

at Bradan and back at Jason.

"*Get home?* You mean he actually lives with you?" Stuart laughed. "Like I said you got sloppy. This is Jason Steed. He works undercover for SYUI and you have him in your home."

"Steed? He's called Jason Norris," Bradan said. "He's just a kid. SYUI wouldn't use a kid."

"He's not a normal kid. He took out two armed British soldiers who were kicking the shite out of me. I was drunk and kept thinking I must have imagined it, but it happened," Shamus said.

Jason took another step forward. He was still in shock of seeing his uncle dealing in explosives with Shamus.

"You little brat." Bradan cursed. "You come into my home and inform on me?" He pulled out a revolver from his back pocket and aimed it at Jason.

Two shots rang out. Jason dived to the ground. He expected to be shot but could feel no pain. He turned and saw Bradan falling backwards. Shamus shouted something and bent down to help his brother. Stuart Steed had drawn his gun and had killed Bradan to save Jason.

Jason slowly picked himself up and looked

at his uncle.

"Bradan!" Shamus screamed, trying to shake life into his brother. He turned and glared at Stuart. "You will die for this." Shamus put his hand on his revolver. Stuart took aim and spoke.

"Shamus, we have done business for years. I don't wish to kill you. If you touch your gun, I will be forced to shoot," Stuart ordered. "I couldn't let Bradan shoot my nephew. Now put your hands up above your head." He gestured with his revolver.

Shamus froze. Slowly, he raised his hands and stood.

"Jason, fetch Bradan and Shamus's guns. Slowly son," Stuart said.

"Um." Jason paused. "You know SYUI will find out about this."

"We will talk later. Safety first. Get the guns," Stuart said.

Shamus glared at Jason as he approached and looked back at Stuart. "Why did you have to shoot Bradan?"

"My dear man, he was going to shoot Jason. One can't have that. After all, blood is thicker than water, and I'm rather fond of the little chap."

Jason picked up Bradan's revolver and took the revolver out of Shamus's back pocket.

"Good boy, Jason, bring them here," Stuart ordered.

Jason thought about keeping them and pointing one at his uncle until SYUI arrived. He considered it, but after seeing his uncle draw his gun and kill Bradan so easily, he doubted he would win a gunfight. Jason knew his own weaknesses. He was not a good shot with a gun. He didn't have time to study the gun. Maybe they had a safety on and would not shoot anyway. No, he would wait. His uncle just saved his life. He would not hurt his only nephew.

Holding the two revolvers by the barrels, Jason carried them back to his uncle.

"So you planted him on Maude and me, why?" Shamus asked. Jason thought Shamus looked just as confused as he was.

"Nothing of the kind Shamus. We would have continued to do business until Scotland Yard Undercover Intelligence's finest, George Young, started sniffing around and sent in his secret weapon, young Jason here."

"So how do you know the little brat?"

"He's my nephew's son. Now, that's enough talking. Jason place them on the seat," Stuart said, pointing at the revolvers he was carrying.

As Jason placed them on the seat, he felt a sharp pain on the back of his head and remembered no more. Stuart had struck him over the back of the head with his own gun.

Stuart looked up across the park's playing field. A police car, two army Land-Rovers, and a car with lights flashing raced towards him. Keeping a watchful eye on Shamus, he bent down and dragged Jason's unconscious body into the back seat of his Jaguar.

"Sorry, I can't stick around, old chap." Stuart scoffed. He jumped into the driver's seat and sped off in the opposite direction.

Shamus was on his knees, sobbing over his dead brother's body. The police forced him onto the ground and placed him in handcuffs. Paddy Murphy and Brenda stepped out and took over the situation. The explosives were found. Shamus was arrested. He later told Brenda and Paddy that SS knew Jason. He even went as far as to say Jason called him uncle.

*

The Reverend Ian Flanagan was arrested for arms dealing. He said the explosives he had were to help the British. The intended victims were the IRA and members such as Shamus O'Neill. Nevertheless, he would get ten years in jail for arms dealing with intent to harm.

CHAPTER FIFTEEN

Jason's back was stiff. His head was thumping with a dull pain. Slowly, he opened his eyes. He was in a kitchen. It was warm and smelt of lavender. It hurt to lift his head. He tried to move his hands and legs; they hurt. He was sat on a wooden chair with his hands behind his back, tied tightly to the back of the chair. Each ankle was tied to a chair leg.

"Ah, Jason dear boy. One was wondering if you were ever going to wake up," Stuart Steed said.

Jason focused on the figure sitting at the table. It was his uncle, sipping a cup of tea.

"My head hurts. What happened?" Jason asked quietly. "Why am I tied up?"

"I've heard all the stories about you Jason. I can't take any risks. Your head is fine, just a small cut. I cleaned it and applied a bandage."

"You hit me?" Jason asked in disbelief.

"Come now Jason, you have had far worse. I couldn't risk you being foolish before I had the chance to explain."

"Where are we?" Jason asked.

"Back in England. You slept for hours. I took a ferry to the Isle of Man and another to England. Your SYUI were probably checking all direct ferry crossings and airports. Not so smart, are they?"

"I…" Jason paused and blinked trying to clear his head. "I need to pee."

Stuart sighed. "Sorry, Jason, you will have to wait."

"But, you can't tie me up. Let me go, Uncle Stuart," Jason said. He struggled against the ropes and bounced around on the chair before resigning to the fact he was tied secure.

"I will call someone in an hour or so to find you. I must explain first. I may not see you again and can't leave it like this," Stuart said.

"Please let me go to the bathroom at least," Jason pleaded. "I really need to go".

His uncle looked annoyed. "One doesn't want to hurt you Jason. If I untie you, please don't try anything or I will be forced to shoot you, maybe not kill you. But nevertheless, it won't be pleasant, I can assure you."

Jason nodded. Stuart cut the ropes behind his back and allowed Jason to untie his legs. Stuart followed him to the bathroom with a revolver pointing in his direction at all times.

When he was done, he was given a mug of tea and some sandwiches to eat. Stuart sat opposite him across the table and watched him eat.

"I don't understand why you would be selling bombs to Bradan and the IRA and how you knew I was here," Jason said, tenderly feeling the bump on his head.

"I didn't, well I gave Shamus the tipoff that George Young was in Belfast. I never thought you would be here until I was at Flanagan's home. I noticed you in a picture with his daughter. That blew your cover. If you want to be a good secret agent, you will need to control your hormones."

"Cailin, she's…" Jason paused. "She's really nice, we just got on well and…" He stopped himself and stared at his uncle. "What were you doing at her home?"

"Her father is a unionist and supplies the union with weapons. He's a customer of mine."

"So you are SS, and you supply the IRA, that's the other side. You supply both sides?" Jason asked.

"I'm not proud of it, but if I don't, someone else will."

"But they killed my grandparents. The IRA and Shamus killed them. That's your own brother and sister-in-law."

Stuart nodded and sipped his tea. "Jason, at age fifty-five I was retired from the army. At fifty–five, they feel you are done. I never married or had a family. I gave my life to the British Army and all I got as a thanks was a pension barely enough to live a measly existence on. I knew of the struggle the Unionists were having in Northern Ireland and met a guy who said he would pay a very high price for small arms. It started off like that, then it went to explosives. The money was incredible, far more than the measly pension the British Government expected me to live on."

"Eventually, my contacts at the army dried up. Tougher controls came, so I sourced arms from overseas, Istanbul in Turkey. Buying from a dealer in Turkey came a hefty price. He agreed to sell to me if I became his main dealer in the UK, so I agreed. The first shipment was twenty pound of gelignite, a nice profit for me until I found out who the buyer was. A young guy called Shamus O'Neill. When I found out he was with the IRA and the explosives would possibly be used on British troops, I refused to sell to him."

"He made threats of course, but I ignored them. They tried to kill me. Unfortunately, your grandparents borrowed my car and used tickets I had been given to an Opera. I can't stand Opera. Can you imagine listening to a ghastly screeching woman singing in Italian? It's not my kind of entertainment, so I gave the tickets to my brother and his wife. Not a single day goes by when I don't wish I could take that back. After the funeral, your father went back to Hong Kong where he was stationed. On that flight, he met your mother.

"A few months later, Shamus appeared with a photograph of your father and mother holding hands, walking down a street in Hong Kong. It was either supply the arms to Shamus or an accident could happen. At first, I refused and was going to warn your father, but your father called me, informing me he was getting married in a hurry, because your mother was expecting a baby, *you*. So I agreed to sell to Shamus. I kept telling myself just this one deal and I would get out.

"As the weeks turned to months and then years, I just carried on being the main supplier. All was going well until I noticed your picture at Flanagan's home. I had to take out some people watching the home, probably SYUI. I called Shamus to sell him what I had. I was going to make it my last deal. Then you showed up, and here we are."

Jason drunk his tea and looked at his uncle. "So you did all this because of my dad and me? Am I supposed to forgive you for having George Young killed or all the British troops that have been killed by your bombs? Uncle Stuart, this is a mess. You will have to tell them you were being blackmailed and were protecting my dad and me," Jason said.

"No, Jason. I killed some agents and much blood has been spilt because of me. I will take you somewhere and drop you off. I have an escape route and plenty of money in safe places.

I'm afraid I must tie you again and blind fold you. I won't hurt you. I would never hurt you. Ever since I first saw you when you were what, four or five, I have loved you. I never had any children. Your father was a fantastic nephew, but when you arrived on the scene, I knew I did the right thing protecting you. You are very special and really have no idea how much one loves you," Stuart said. Jason noticed his uncle had tears in his eyes.

*

For three hours, Jason travelled in the back seat of the car wearing a blindfold. Eventually, the car stopped. Stuart stepped out and opened the back door. He pulled Jason out and removed his blindfold. Jason squinted while his eyes adjusted to the bright light. He was on the edge of a wooded area parked down a deserted country lane. He could smell cow manure. He glanced across the field; a tractor pulled a trailer, spitting out manure. A flock of seagulls followed it, diving in to pick up worms that were chased out as the soil was churned.

"Where are we?" Jason asked.

"Just over the hill you will see Tiverton. You're in Devon. Here, take this so you can make a call at a phone box," Stuart said, passing Jason some coins.

"I'm not sure why I don't hate you and take you down. I'm not a very good secret agent am I?" Jason said glumly.

"Nonsense, you are the best agent Britain has, but when it comes to family, your loyalties are divided."

"George Young was a friend. Bradan was a terrorist and had blood on his hands. I don't care about him. But all the British troops that got hurt in Northern Ireland by weapons you traded is unforgiveable," Jason said.

"You will find it in your heart to forgive me. That's a promise," Stuart said. He leant forward, kissed Jason's forehead, and then climbed back into the car. He lowered the window down and smiled at Jason.

"No, I will never forgive you. I will find you Uncle Stuart, that's a promise. And when I do, you will have to pay for your crimes and for treason against our country. The thing that upsets me the most is Dad looks up to you and you've let him down," Jason said.

"That's a good attitude, my boy. You should despise me more. Curse me more and hate me with every molecule of your soul! Then, you should use that hatred to survive what the world throws at you." Jason was left in a cloud of exhaust fumes.

The walk to Tiverton took Jason just over an hour. Most of the time, he regretted not trying to disarm his uncle and call SYUI. On the other hand, he felt proud that his uncle saved his life when Bradan was going to shoot him. The strong smell of manure followed him. It reminded him of a few years earlier when he was in the country with his grandparents and he had complained about farm manure smell. His grandmother told him the smell would give him rosy red cheeks.

He came across a phone box and called SYUI in London. Once he gave his name, an officer took his details. Within five minutes, three police cars greeted him at the phone box. They were given instructions to pick him up and keep him safe. Devon and Cornwall Police didn't often get orders from SYUI. It became a priority, but they were unsure why this boy was so important and not sure if he was a criminal or just a runaway boy. They were unsure whether to put him in a cell or interview room. They settled to watching him in the canteen where he sat and watched TV. He was eventually picked up by SYUI and taken back to London.

*

Brenda and Scott arrived back in London the following day. Jason gave his statements to

SYUI. The only help he could give them regarding the cottage he was held at was that he could hear the ocean and knew it was about a three hour drive to Tiverton. But that didn't help much, and Stuart Steed could have been driving in circles to confuse Jason.

Ray Steed was upset hearing the news regarding his uncle. Brenda broke the news to him. He was furious that Jason was knocked unconscious by his uncle. Ray felt guilty and just as much embarrassed by the situation as Jason was. Jason missed Cailin more than he let anyone know. He wondered how she would be coping without her father and how she would cope with the news that her father was dealing in arms. Jason buried himself in karate. He worked out harder than he ever had before.

He woke at six in the morning and ran around the grounds of his home before performing karate katas on the front lawns. The tennis machine was dug out of the shed. He used the remote to turn it on and stood in front of it, blocking the balls as they fired at terrific speed in his direction. Having it set on random improved his reactions. All went well until he deflected one ball and it took out a window above the front door.

Brenda arrived again at his home. He noticed her talking to his father so he kept his distance. An hour later, her car was still parked on the driveway. He was annoyed she was still at his home as he entered to get a drink.

"Jason, how are you holding up?" Brenda asked.

"Fine."

Brenda looked at Ray, both looked at Jason.

"Is something wrong Jase?" his father asked.

"No."

"We are going to wrap up the case. Shamus will go to jail, probably for the rest of his life," Brenda said. "Maude was an accomplice but we have no evidence to prosecute her."

"What will happen to the Flanagan family?" Jason asked.

"We have frozen the bank accounts. Most of the money was from arms deals. Even the home could be taken. But I'm sure Mrs. Flanagan and her children will be fine, and Cailin is a strong girl. She will recover from her two losses," Brenda said.

"Two losses? What else happened?" Jason asked concerned.

"Well Jason, she will miss her father who will be in prison and of course the boy she knew as Jason Norris." Brenda smirked.

"Cailin, that's a pretty name," Ray said.

"And you Jason, did you get over her?" Brenda asked.

Jason paused and looked at her. She was being nice, more relaxed, not the battle-axe he had first met. She was warmer towards him now she was off the case. He ignored the question. Deep down, he missed her but knew he would never see her again.

CHAPTER SIXTEEN

Scott came to spend the weekend at Jason's home. As usual, he slept the night on a pullout mattress next to Jason's bed. Although they never got to sleep until the early hours of the morning, they talked about girls, joked, farted as much as they could, and ate so much chocolate and soda they felt sick before finally falling to sleep.

Jason decided to skip his workout in the morning. He woke at just after nine and scrambled to the edge of his bed and looked down at Scott.

"You awake?" Jason asked.

Scott opened his eyes and looked up at Jason and laughed. "Your hair looks like you have been struck by lightning. Why don't you cut it shorter?"

Jason licked his palm and tried to flatten it. "I like it long on the front, besides girls like it."

"Do you miss Cailin?" Scott asked.

"Yeah, the undercover stuff is okay, but when you get close to people it's hard knowing you will never see them again. Even Gober was kinda cool in his own way."

"You mean *Gobnait O'Grady.*" Scott laughed. He sat up on one elbow and looked at Jason. "Are you going to come back to St Joseph's School now?"

"I really wanted to go back to the military school in America, but I don't think they would have me back after last time. Although Dad was gonna ask. Do you want some toast?"

"Yeah."

"I'll get it," Jason said, jumping out of bed.

He arrived back in five minutes with a tray of toast and three mugs of tea.

"Mrs. Beeton made it. I'll take a tea in to Dad," Jason said. He plodded down the hallway carrying a mug of tea and entered his father's bedroom.

"Wakey-wakey, Dad. I got you a mug of tea. Did you contact the military school yet? Can I go back?" Jason said before looking up. He froze in his tracks. The bed had two lumps, giving the outline of two people. He noticed his father's clothing and a woman's clothing on the floor.

"Oh," Jason said sheepishly. "I only brought one tea." He placed it were he stood on the floor, too embarrassed to go any further.

His father lifted himself up and looked at him. "Can you bring an extra tea please, Jason?" He looked at the person lying next to him. Jason was still unsure who it was. "Do you take sugar?"

Brenda lifted herself up and looked at Jason. She held the covers to her neck to keep herself covered. "Morning Jason. No I don't take sugar."

Jason nodded and left as fast as he could, running back to his bedroom and jumping into his bed as if it was a safe sanctuary.

"Scott, you are not going to believe this. I don't think I believe it myself," Jason said. Scott was munching on the toast.

"What?"

"Battle Axe is here, and it looks like she's been here all night. You'll never guess where she slept." Jason said.

"With your dad," Scott said as a matter of fact.

"You don't seem surprised?" Jason said, taken back.

"They were pretty close last night. Didn't you see the way your dad looked at her?"

"No, I thought he was just being nice to her."

"Well, looks like Battle Axe could be your stepmother." Scott laughed.

"No way, she already said that SYUI won't

be using me on any missions as I'm too young." Jason sat heavily on the floor next to Scott. He had never seen his father with a lady before. It had just been the two of them and the housekeeper Mrs. Beeton. He thought about the prospect of having a stepmother and even the possibility of a younger brother or sister, before dismissing the idea. No, they were just adult friends he told himself.

Jason and Scott spent Saturday coming up with a list of people to invite to Jason's upcoming thirteenth birthday party. He decided to invite Princess Catherine and a few from St Joseph's School. He would also invite Brenda now that she was close to his father. He would call his grandparents in Scotland and ask if they could come down. Scott's parents, a couple of friends from sea cadets, and one from his karate class. It would seem strange not having his Uncle Stewart.

Monday, he returned to St. Joseph's. It had been nearly five months since he last attended. In between, he had been to the American military school and of course the school in Belfast while under cover. His blazer and tie still fit, but he needed larger shirts and pants.

His previous arrangement of taking extra language classes and forgoing physical activity was allowed again as long as he continued with

Judo and Karate. Scott was delighted to have his best friend back as school with him.

*

Jason's grandparents came down for his thirteenth birthday party. Jason enjoyed seeing family and some friends at his home, but the party was awkward. He was too old for balloons, party games, and toys, yet not old enough to drink. They mostly sat around eating, with Scott telling jokes. The adults stayed in the hallway drinking and talking while the boys sat in the living room and played a game of truth or dare when Ray called Jason.

"Jason, you have another guest coming. You may want to meet this one yourself."

Jason was sat on the floor with his other friends. He lifted himself to his feet and came out into the hallway. His grandmother caught him and fussed with his hair.

"Tuck your shirt in, Jason, and put your shoes on," she scolded in her Scottish accent.

"I'm not going out," Jason said. He glanced out the front door. A black Rolls Royce pulled up outside the house. A smile ran across his face. He walked out barefoot onto the drive.

Princess Catherine stepped out of the back. She wore a tight fitting black dress and carried a gift and a card. She mirrored his grin when she saw him.

They gave each other an awkward kiss and looked at each other.

"I didn't think you would come. You never replied to my invitation, and it was a bit short notice," Jason said.

"It was either visit a new maternity ward with my mother that she is opening or come here and see you. Looks like you won," Catherine said. "One wasn't sure what to wear; you never mentioned it. Jason, if you invite me, I *need* to know stuff like that."

"You look great. I like your dress. You look so…" He paused, trying to find the right words as he looked her up and down trying not to be too obvious in areas where she was growing. "Mature."

Catherine smiled. Her dress was lower than she would normally wear but now she was getting older could wear it comfortably. "Should I leave my shoes in the car?" she joked.

Jason laughed at her and took her hand. "No, we were sat on the floor playing truth or dare. Sorry, it's all boys apart from the adults."

"Truth or dare?" She said it so it sounded like a question.

"Yeah." Jason laughed. "But we will have to stop that now you are here. Some of the stuff my friends reveal isn't really the type of thing you would want to hear. It's boys stuff and pretty gross."

Jason and Catherine stayed together most of the time. Scott stayed with the other boys. Catherine caught Jason staring at her.

"What are you looking at?" she asked.

"I've missed you and forgot how..." He stopped trying to get the courage to say what he wanted to without sounding foolish. "I forgot how pretty you are in person. We haven't seen much of each other and drifted apart."

"I still feel the same about you, Jason. You have grown a little too. And it's the first time we've spoken face to face now your voice has broken. I know it's hard for us, and it won't get any easier the older we get. The media would love to take pictures of us together and would say sorts of stuff about us. I still consider you as my boyfriend and would never go out with anyone else."

She paused before continuing forlornly. "My mother does not realize that as much as she tries to keep you at a distance from me, it will not lesson my deep affection for you."

"Good, then I'll find a way to hang around and annoy her for a long time."

"Would you ever go out with anyone else?" she questioned.

Jason looked down and quickly forced himself to look at her in the eyes. "Good, I feel the same. I wouldn't go out with anyone else myself." As soon as he said it, he felt guilty. He had grown close to Cailin and had enjoyed kissing her. He tried to convince himself that Cailin was just part of the mission, but he could never tell Catherine. The worst part was he still missed Cailin and when he was with her he enjoyed himself. Now he was with Catherine, he was just as happy but confused.

After a few hours, his friends started to leave. Jason walked Catherine round to the side of the house away from prying eyes.

"Why did we come here?" Catherine asked.

"Your chauffer was watching, and I'm sure my gran will be watching," Jason said.

"She is really sweet." Catherine held both Jason's hands and looked at him. His deep sapphire blue eyes burnt into her. She was lost in him, the same emotion she felt when she had first seen him. They shared a private moment for few minutes before returning to the front of the house holding hands. He thanked her for coming and his gift, a silver necklace with a cross.

He walked into his home and was greeted by Scott. "So how did she get over the news about you and Cailin?" Scott teased.

"She was happy for me and surprised I only had one girlfriend," he said before his smile changed to a serious look. "I didn't tell her. Cailin was just a girl I met on a mission that doesn't count. I forgot how much I like Catherine."

"You know if she ever finds out, they will send you to the Tower of London and lock you up, probably cut off your lips so you can't kiss another girl. Maybe cut something else off too." Scott laughed.

Brenda interrupted the two boys. "Jason, I heard you and Princess Catherine were friends, but until today I never knew you were *that* type of friend. I'm impressed. She seems really taken by you. You seem to have girls all over England and Ireland fancying you."

"Why of course, just look at what they get." Jason laughed, flexing his arms in a muscle man pose.

"Huh typical boy. Well be careful; girls at her age can be hurt," Brenda said.

"Yes mum," Jason said as a joke but wanted to get his father's reaction who was in ear shot.

Ray smiled and said nothing.

CHAPTER SEVENTEEN

Jason's life soon got back to normal. After school, Jason attended sea cadets. His recent missions meant he had been at different schools learning new subjects and syllabuses. He had slipped further behind the rest of his class. It didn't help matters when they took mid-term exams. He hadn't been at school to learn the history project on Oliver Cromwell and the English civil war. The consequence was he came bottom in history. He had been average at math but had slipped behind St Joseph's high standard.

Jason soon found himself where he was some six months earlier, struggling at a school he hated. Scott's brilliance at all subjects compounded the matter, and Jason actually resented Scott who would immediately throw his arm up at any question asked in the classroom.

Raymond Steed was given a promotion from Lieutenant Commander to Commander and given a shore-based position in Portsmouth. The promotion meant he would be home most weekends. Jason was happier, but Ray now spent much of his spare time with Brenda. Jason tried to hide his ill feelings towards her and keep them to himself. On one hand, he was happy for his father. On the other, Brenda was always in his home. Rather than come across as an angry teenager, he took his frustration out by deeply submersing himself in martial arts.

Jason continued to train hard. The tennis machine firing balls at him on full speed was no longer a challenge. He had his father purchase him another and set them up facing each other some thirty feet apart. He stood in direct line of both machines, and as they spat out balls one after another, he blocked the balls, sending them in all directions.

Occasionally, he could be heard cursing at himself when he had missed and been caught in the face or body by one of the tennis balls. Mrs.

Beeton, the housekeeper, was concerned about Jason's behavior. She tried mentioning it to Ray who shrugged it off as a phase he was going through.

When help came, it was from the last person Jason would suspect, but he welcomed it.

Ray came home for the weekend and booked a table at an Indian Restaurant. He would take Brenda and Jason out for dinner. Jason said nothing in the car on the journey over. If he was spoken to, he simply grunted a few replies.

"Jason did you get that black eye from the tennis machines?" Ray asked, gently touching the side of his sons face.

"Yeah."

"And the bruises on the back of your hands?"

"Yeah."

"Isn't that a little extreme son? And don't just give me a *yeah* or no."

"How else can I train? I want to improve," Jason snapped.

"Why do you need to, aren't you good

enough already?"

"No, I can now defend myself from two tennis machines. Imagine that was two or four people attacking me. I have fast reactions. Wong Tong said you must embrace your gift. My gift is my speed." Jason said. He enjoyed talking about karate. It was the most words he had said to his father in a long while.

Brenda cut in. "You're not happy at school, are you Jason?"

"I hate it. I can't spend another five years doing that. I will leave school at sixteen," Jason said as a matter of fact.

"What, sixteen? No you'll stay until you are eighteen and graduate. From there, you can go to college or if you still want a military career, you can join as an officer cadet in the Navy. Or, of course, if you prefer Marines, Army, or Air-Force," Ray said.

"I can join the Navy at sixteen," Jason argued.

"That is for regular crew, not officers. You will train as an officer when you leave at eighteen."

"I would leave school now if I could. I

hate it. Stupid teachers who have done nothing but go to college and become teachers. They think they know it all. They haven't been shot or seen friends killed or injured. None of them have fought for the country, slept in a jungle, or under a tree. What can they teach me? Nothing. I *will* be leaving school at sixteen. Legally, I'm allowed."

Ray looked in his rear view mirror at Jason and glared at his son. "I'm not arguing with you tonight, Jason. We are going out for a nice meal. We will talk about it later."

"Fine, but when I'm sixteen I'm joining," Jason said folding his arms and making sure he had the last word.

During the meal, Jason said nothing. He picked at his food and looked miserable.

"Actually, I have a suggestion that may work, and before you both snap at me, let me finish," Brenda said. Both Ray and Jason nodded.

She held Rays hand and placed her other hand on top of it. "Ray, I'm not blind. Jason is not happy with his school he hates it, and I don't blame him."

"What?" Ray said before Brenda put her finger to his lips to shut him up.

"Ray, the poor boy has been used. George Young used him on mission after mission. You even allowed him to go undercover to find a runaway girl. And let's not forget when you were captured, he flew half way around the world to get you out, and he did it alone. He just came off another mission and learnt his uncle is an arms dealer. He witnessed George Young and Bradan O'Neill getting shot in front of him. He took on a group of thugs, and with Scotts' help, worked out who was smuggling guns and explosives."

"In return, we send him to a private boy's school that he hated long before he went to the American military academy," Brenda said before Jason interrupted her.

"I liked it at the military school," Jason said.

"Jason isn't like other boys. He can fly a plane, kill with a single punch, take on four or five adults, and has seen more death and destruction than any adult should see. Putting him at St. Joseph's School is like using a thoroughbred racehorse to give kiddies donkey rides or like trying to use a fighter jet to spray crops."

Jason was surprised by Brenda's words, but he welcomed them. "It's nice to be referred to as a fighter jet or a racehorse." He smiled. "See

Dad, even Brenda agrees St Joseph's School is a dump."

"No, that is not what I said Jason. It's a very good school and expensive, but any normal school you go to will be difficult for you." Brenda paused. She took a large sip of wine and placed her hand back on Rays. "I have something to suggest. I was going to leave it until after the weekend, but now is as good a time as any."

Ray and Jason looked at her waiting to hear more.

"I know I said unlike George Young I would never use Jason on a mission. Well I wouldn't. Two days ago the Americans, well the CIA to be precise, contacted SYUI. They requested a little help from us," Brenda said.

Jason's face lit up. His right knee uncontrollably bounced up and down at a rapid pace while he waited with anticipation to hear more.

"Ray, I also made a promise to you I would never use him on a mission. I intend to keep that promise. MI6 were very interested in Jason's statements regarding Stuart Steed. They shared some with the CIA. We now know that his contact was in Turkey. Istanbul, to be exact. Turkey borders Iran, Iraq, and Greece. For years,

MI6 and the CIA have suspected weapons, bomb making equipment, and even military vehicles pass into Europe via Turkey.

"We suspect this is where Stuart Steed and others bought weapons from. The CIA have several suspects in Istanbul. They supply the likes of Stuart Steed who was supplying to military organizations in Northern Ireland. But Stuart was a small player. Others include rebels in Africa including ivory poachers, General Gaddafi in Liberia, and Palestine terrorists. The C.I.A. are planting an undercover team in Istanbul next month. A male and female agent posing as teachers at IICS, Istanbul International Community School. To help with their cover, they requested that they had a child who will also attend the school as a pupil."

"IICS is one of the oldest schools in the world. Its students come from around the world. Jason would fit right in. Language is a huge part of the educational system. He would be mixing with German, Chinese, Japanese, Swiss, French, and Middle Eastern students. Of course some British also attend. The standard is very good. I doubt you would be bored, Jason."

"What would be my role?" Jason asked.

"No role. You go to school and come home to an apartment after school with your fake parents. You don't do anything. This is a huge CIA operation. I don't want you to do any snooping around, just go to school, make friends, and have a nice time. It could last months. If you like the school after the mission is over, maybe you could stay as a boarder."

They are not yet married and already the wicked stepmother wants to send me away Jason thought.

"It seems pointless. They don't need me. They could take any kid." Jason shrugged.

"Not really. There's a one in a million chance something goes wrong. The CIA would prefer to have Jason Steed as the child of the CIA couple rather than a regular kid," Brenda said.

Jason looked at Ray, trying to guess his response. So far, he had said nothing. "Brenda, are you sure? Jason is just a school boy who, if something should go wrong, is able to take care of him? I don't want him in harm's way with the type of people you mentioned," Ray asked.

Brenda gently squeezed Ray's hand. "I can't promise you that. I have been given only what they want SYUI to know. The CIA agents are going in as teachers who are also a married couple with a child. Having a schoolboy with them makes them look normal. They will be teaching English and math. The school itself is famous and has a great syllabus. Jason will be mixing with mostly the children of wealthy parents who either work in Turkey or are there because of the school's academic achievements."

"Still sounds boring, but if I can help the CIA I would like to. When I'm older, and if I start working for MI6, then it will be good to have friends in the CIA."

"MI6? I thought you wanted to join the Navy and later the SAS?" Ray asked.

"Yeah to start with, but MI6 go all over the world and take on the likes of the Russian KGB. That sounds much more interesting, and MI6 agents are allowed to carry a gun," Jason said.

"So are SYUI officers," Brenda argued.

"No disrespect, but SYUI are just the Intelligence force of the police. Scott said MI6 get paid more, see more action, *and* can carry a gun. He wants to work for them as well in the intelligence department. So we could still be friends and work together," Jason said.

Ray smiled and nodded. "You seem to have it worked out, but for now, Istanbul? I need to know more details before I let Jason go."

CHAPTER EIGHTEEN

Two weeks later, Jason sat alone waiting, in a private lounge at London's Heathrow airport. He flicked through World Karate magazine stopping every now and then to read articles he found interesting. After an hour, he grew bored and decided to take a walk around the airport. As he tried to leave the lounge, outside the door was a well-built man with a bald head who stood in his way.

Jason looked up at him. He looked around thirty. Although he was wearing a dark suit, Jason thought he looked muscular. His arms filled out his jacket. His chest stuck out several inches more than his waist.

"Sorry son, you have to stay here out of sight," the man said in an American accent.

"I'm bored and thirsty. Can I go and get a Coke?" Jason asked, trying to peer around the large man.

"My orders are to keep you out of sight and make sure no one comes in or out."

"What if I need to pee?" Jason asked.

"Then I can escort you to the bathroom and back," he said.

"Awesome, then escort me to the Coke machine." Jason smiled and pushed passed. He walked a few paces and checked to see if he was being followed. He noticed the large American following him, Jason slowed down and walked alongside him. "So do you work for the CIA?"

"I work for my country."

"Want one?" Jason asked as he fed the vending machine with a ten pence coin.

The large man looked around to see if he was being watched and looked back at Jason. "Sure, thanks."

Safely back in the private lounge, the man opened up a little to Jason. He was called Chuck and explained he was a US marine and was recruited to Special Forces. Jason told him of the time he had spent at the American military school.

It was another hour before a knock came at the door. Chuck responded cautiously and opened it. He stepped outside. Jason waited. A minute later, a couple walked in with luggage. They looked Jason up and down and smiled.

Jason took mental notes of them. The woman looked around forty, slim and athletic. She had dark shoulder length hair that had a tinge of grey covering it. She had intelligent, watchful eyes and a thin pointed nose. The man looked a similar age. Apart from some short black hair above his eyes that circled around the back of his head, he was bald. He was slim and seemed very confident. He strode towards Jason and held out his hand with a warm smile.

"Jason Steed, I presume," he said. Jason nodded. "I'm..." He paused and looked back at the woman. "I'm Dad, although it sounds strange saying that. I'll be known as Dexter Delong. This is Mom, and she will be known as Karen Delong, and you will use the same surname." Jason shook her hand as well.

"My real mum was called Karen," Jason said.

"Oh wow, you do sound English," Karen said. "Nice to meet you, Jason."

"Derrrr. What did you expect, Chinese?" Jason asked. "I'm British. I sound British."

"And he's witty too. No doubt you also come with angry teenager tantrums and loud music." She looked at Jason with a calm expression. There was no emotion in her voice.

"First impressions and we're off to a good start then." Jason grinned. Dexter checked his watch and gestured Jason to take a seat. He explained in great detail that, from this point on, Jason was only to call him Dad and Karen was to be Mom. They would be catching a flight in an hour to Istanbul, Turkey. He went over the mission twice. Jason's job was to go to school and come home and act like any other kid.

Karen cut in. "They gave us a file on you Jason, quite impressive. Queens Award for bravery, you have a pilot's license, and were involved in the rescue after the Jakarta massacre and the UN team held in Vietnam."

"The CIA have a file on me?" Jason asked, trying to conceal his excitement.

"It's not all good. You assaulted four military police officers that needed hospital treatment at Camp Pendleton and had your entire academy banned from the military games for a year. You went AWOL and disobeyed orders that came indirectly from the president. You have also had your fair share of 'run-ins' with the Brits, assaulting a teenager that blew your cover on a mission."

"On this case you *will* obey orders from Karen and myself at all times, no heroics. If you even think about hitting someone, you will be on the first plane back to Britain and on assault charges," Dexter said.

Jason studied Dexter. Everything about him was imposing, from his immaculate black suit to his jet-black hair with grey streaks just above his ears.

"The teenager had a knife and tried to mug me. I would do the same again. And I was defending fellow cadets at Pendleton and was defending myself against four or five of them when one threw grit in my eyes. I couldn't see. When the military police came and tried to grab me, I thought I was still being attacked," Jason argued.

"Ah he has excuses. And going AWOL? Were you under attack again?" Karen sniggered.

Jason stood and faced her. "No, but if I didn't my father and many others would be dead now. I would do the same again. I don't know about you, but *I* love my family and put them first. You can put that in your file in bold letters."

"Oh yes family like, what's his name? Stuart Steed." Karen sneered.

Jason took a step forward, before taking a breath and turning away trying to calm himself down.

Dexter smiled at Jason and nodded. "I could almost see that temper of yours emerge then. A Mr. George Young wrote in your file 'anyone should stand clear when Jason loses his temper.' Is it that bad?"

He sat down heavily in his seat again. "It's not good. I'm trying to control it," Jason said and looked down at the floor. "George was killed on our last mission." Thinking about George dying was still very painful for Jason. He partly blamed himself for not getting to George and Scott in time.

"If you just go to school and be a school boy on this mission, you'll be fine," Dexter said.

Jason liked Dexter, he reminded him of an American movie star who always said and did the right thing. As for Karen, he was still unsure about her.

*

His first impression of Istanbul International Airport was as he expected. A crowded modern building with a mixture of businessmen and tourists carrying suitcases and rushing in all directions. Some looked lost, others impatiently tutted and walked around people who stopped to read the overhead directional signs.

The taxicab driver sang while driving the makeshift Delong family. His cab had no air-conditioning. It took an hour before stopping outside a modern four-story apartment block in the city. Jason stretched as he climbed out, trying to get his muscles to come back to life. It was early evening and still hot. Jason thought the heat was coming from the ground. The sidewalk had been baking all day. The whole area felt dry and extremely hot.

He collected his case and followed Karen and Dexter inside the building. The apartment had a marble tile floor throughout, a modern leather sofa, and a large television. His bedroom was small, but clean. He bounced down on the bed and kicked off his shoes and socks. Dexter knocked on his door and walked in.

"Can I come in?" he asked. Walking in Jason's room he noticed Jason's questionable look but ignored it. "Put your shoes on we'll go out and eat."

After a nice meal at a restaurant in the town center, Jason sat quietly. He had noticed Dexter briefly talk to a man as they arrived. The man was older, maybe sixty, dressed in an immaculate suit and gleaming black polished shoes that looked out of place. He had white hair and a white beard. Jason thought in the winter the man could pass as Santa Claus.

Dexter ordered another bottle of wine for

himself and Karen. It surprised Jason; Dexter requested a certain year of Chardonnay. A tight knot started to form in the pit of Jason's stomach. At first, he tried to ignore it, but something was wrong with the situation. He had always trusted his instincts and his gut feeling. It was poking him with enough force to cause a hibernating grizzly bear to waken from its deep sleep.

Dexter poured himself and Karen another glass of wine. Jason finished his Coke and placed his glass down heavily on the table. He noticed the watch on Dexter's wrist. A Rolex, but not just any Rolex. This was Gold and had diamonds as hour markers.

"That's a nice watch," Jason said causally.

Dexter smiled and pulled his shirtsleeve down over it. "It's nothing too special. Do you want desert? I can ask for the menu. They may even have carrot cake."

"Wow you have done your homework, sure yes please. I'll never turn down carrot cake," Jason said.

Karen made small talk and complained about the cab ride from the airport. She felt all taxicabs should have air-conditioning fitted by law. Jason took notice of everyone around. The waiter had an acne scared face and greasy skin. The couple at the next table were French; he had heard them speak. An older couple a few tables away had glanced at Jason a few times.

Am I being paranoid? Jason asked himself. No the watch, the wine, Dexter's clothing. Even Karen's suitcase was Louis Vuitton. If they were CIA, surely they would not be earning the kind of money to buy them. Dexter noticed Jason was looking around the room. He was sat on the edge of his chair, and he had stopped eating.

"What's wrong Jason?" Dexter asked.

"Nothing."

"Sure there is. You haven't touched your carrot cake, and according to your file, you love it. You seem on edge."

Jason looked at him, not sure what to say. He was annoyed with himself for giving his anxiety away so easily.

"It's nothing, maybe a little nervous about a new school," Jason said. He looked at Karen who was studying him. "I'm fine, Karen."

Dexter and Karen looked at each other. The fact they never corrected him when he called her Karen made his theory all the more real.

Jason watched as Dexter poured himself another glass of wine and drunk it back. "I thought it was Scott who was the smart one? Seems you are smarter than we thought. All will become clear tomorrow at school."

"So until then I have to just trust you?" Jason said, raising his eyebrows.

"Trust, it is us who have to trust you Jason. After all, your uncle is a known arms dealer who supplied terrorists, A Mr. Bradan O'Neill was shot in your presence, and you say you were knocked out and later released but had no idea where you were held? How do we know you are not part of it and we can actually trust you?" Karen asked. "Strange how you can take on four or five military police who are used to handling US Marines and yet now a retired army major knocks you out?"

"He hit me over the head with a gun. I wasn't expecting it, and then he tied me up. You are twisting it and making it sound like I'm a criminal. You can stick that idea where the monkey sticks its nuts," Jason said, raising his voice. He stood up from the table.

"Okay Jason relax, sit down," Dexter said, waving his hand down at Jason. "Please Jason, sit down. Your reaction is enough to tell me I can trust you. We are on the same side. Finish your carrot cake and let's go home. Tomorrow, everything will be explained."

Jason slowly sat down in his chair. He thought for a while. If Dexter or Karen had wanted to hurt him they could have done that at anytime. He had fallen asleep on the plane or they could have done something at the apartment. For now, he would play along and see where it would lead them. He wondered if Brenda had known about any of this. No, she really cared for his father. Although it made him cringe every time they kissed in front of him, she genuinely loved his father.

*

Jason lay in bed, trying to fight off sleep and put the pieces together. Eventually, like a thick fog, tiredness crept over him and smothered his tired body, and he was asleep.

In the moning Dexter knocked on his door and poked his head in. "Jason, time to get up. We have to be at the school in an hour."

Jason lifted himself up onto one elbow. "What's the point of you bloody knocking if you come in anyway?" Jason grunted.

"Ah early morning teenager. I heard the teenage species were angry in the morning,"

Dexter said happily with a broad smile that made Jason even angrier.

"I might have been getting dressed or something." Jason frowned, swinging his legs out from under the covers and onto the floor.

Dexter left whistling to himself, leaving the door wide open. That provoked Jason more. He plodded out of bed to use the bathroom and found the door locked.

"Karen's in the shower. She won't be long. I made you a coffee," Dexter shouted from the kitchen.

Jason walked into the kitchen and slumped down at the table. "Have you got tea?"

"Tea? No, I'm American. Here get this down, you'll feel better." Dexter smiled passing him a coffee.

"Are you *always* so happy in the mornings?" Jason asked, looking down at his reflection in his coffee before taking a sip. He noticed his hair was sticking up in all directions, and his pajama top had come unbuttoned. He slowly fiddled with his buttons and did himself up.

"Why, sure. It's a beautiful day, another

wonderful day God has given us," Dexter said, passing Jason some toast.

Jason ignored him. Karen came out of the bathroom. She wore a black skirt, white blouse, and smelt of perfume that was so strong it tainted the taste of Jason's coffee.

*

Later, as they left the apartment, Karen and Dexter walked ahead. Jason sluggishly followed, his hair still wet from his shower. Dexter used a key to open the door of a white Anadol A1 car. The Istanbul International Community School board had provided the Turkish built car for the family to use.

"What is it with this country? Haven't they heard of AC?" Karen complained examining the cars controls.

"I guess not," Dexter said.

The journey took under ten minutes through the busy streets of Istanbul. Jason marveled at the scenes. Brightly painted trams packed with commuters twisted a path through the traffic. Women wearing traditional burka's many black, some in groups wearing blue burka's. He noticed a child wearing one; he assumed it was a young girl. He wondered how hot it would be to wear one. The garment was like a long dress that dragged on the floor and covered the head. There was a small opening in the front for the woman to see out.

Some men sat on street corners selling newspapers, others sold what Jason thought looked like dried meat. In among the scene, young men raced past on mopeds, wearing modern western clothing. It was a strange mix and looked like a battle of time-honored clothing and traditions against modern influences from the western world.

"Ah here we are, Istanbul Community School," Dexter said. He parked the car and swung around in his seat to look at Jason. "Be good Jason. Remember, this is not a mission for you. Make friends and be a normal boy, learn something."

Jason's attention was drawn outside to a group of three girls his age who walked past. One glanced back and took a second look at Jason. "Yeah, I may like it here." He was given a timetable and a backpack.

"What's in it?" Jason asked, swinging it over his shoulder.

"Everything you will need. Now run along, your first lesson starts in five minutes,"

Dexter said.

The brick built building stood four stories tall. A set of granite steps led up to double doors that were held open by large brass hooks. He looked down at the timetable and smiled when he read the subjects. Science, Math, World History, English, French, German, Spanish, Turkish, Music, Horticulture, and Physical Education. Jason enjoyed foreign languages. He excelled in French, German, and Spanish. He was looking forward to learning Turkish.

He slowly walked along the corridor; boys and girls from a few years younger to a few years older walked around him. He followed his timetable and the room numbers. His first lesson was Horticulture, something he hadn't done before. Eventually, he found room 1G. The room was empty. He stopped and double-checked his timetable and the room number before walking in. It was marked 1G Horticulture and in brackets it was marked *door at the end*. He assumed that it was because the class was at the end of the corridor on its own.

The walls were decorated with pictures of various crops, farm animals, and tractors. At the end of the wall was a huge picture map of the world. Jason looked at it, trying to pick out the countries. Australia and New Zealand were dotted with sheep. Brazil had chocolate bars. The

United States was represented with corn, sugar beet, and tobacco. He didn't notice the door in the very corner open until a lady stepped out.

"Jason?" she asked in an accent. Jason couldn't make out if it was Russian or German.

"Em, yes ma'am. Am I the only one in the class?" Jason asked.

"What does your timetable say?" she asked, pointing a ruler at him.

He looked at it again. "Room 1G, *the door at the end*. I think I'm right," he said.

She tutted and held the ruler at arm's length and pointed it at him like it was a wand. "At the end of this ruler is an idiot, don't you agree?" She sneered.

"If you mean the end facing you, I can't say for sure. I hardly know you." Jason grinned.

"Are you always a smartass?" she sneered.

"Nope, just around idiots."

Her eyes glared at him, trying to bury themselves deep into his soul. "I heard you were over-confident, bad-tempered, and abrasive. Seems our sources were right to warn us of your flaws as well as your skills. Follow me," she said, swiftly turning and going into the door in the corner of the room. Jason followed and paused at the door. She stood inside a small six-foot square room with shelving full of books and paper.

"It's a…" He paused in disbelief. "A storage closet."

"It's the door at the end room. Come in and close the door behind you," she snapped. Jason slowly entered and pulled the door shut behind him. With it closed, she pushed a stack of books back and the whole wall slid back. Jason's mouth opened wide, not sure what to say. A corridor opened up. The cool, damp air made Jason's skin prickle.

"What's this?" he asked.

"Don't ask me. After all, you think *I'm* an idiot," she snapped. "Come on, we haven't got all day."

Jason stood where he was. He took in his surroundings. She looked about fifty, slim, with grey hair tied up behind her head. She wore black pants with a matching black top. It had a logo in the center with what Jason thought looked like a map of the world. The corridor was built of brick; the floor was a grey concrete. The lights that illuminated the corridor looked old; the bulbs hung in large metal hangers.

The woman noticed Jason was not following and glared at him again. "So the famous Jason Steed is nervous?" she scoffed.

"No, he's just not stupid. Where does this go? And my name is Delong; Jason Delong," he said, although as soon as he said it, he knew it was pointless. She obviously knew who he was.

She smiled at him and sighed. "Jason I know who you are and you are no more Jason DeLong than I'm Miss World."

"I dunno, you might have looked quite hot in a swimsuit a hundred years ago. Where does this go? You're right, I'm nervous. Who are you?" Jason said, slowly walking forward. He was not accustomed to feeling nervous, but he could not suppress the prickling sense of unease that was creeping over him.

"You have nothing to fear, Jason. Follow me," she said. Her heels clicked as she walked off down the corridor.

He followed as she marched ahead. Jason's stomach knotted as another twinge of apprehension washed over him. The corridor turned. Jason was certain he was going down, and by the cooler temperature, knew it was underground. She stopped at a large steel door. The same logo, a picture of the world, was painted on the front. She punched some numbers in the keypad next to the door and opened it.

It opened up into a brightly lit, modern corridor. The air was warmer, and he could hear people's voices. He followed her down the corridor. Each room it passed had glass windows. Inside, people were working; many stopped and stared when they saw him, some pointing and talking about him. They all wore the same black uniform with logo.

After a flight of stairs, they came to what Jason could only describe as the inside of a large office block. A man walked past and smiled. "Hello, Jason," he said. Jason recognized him. It was the man with the Santa beard who spoke to Dexter the night before at the restaurant. Jason's mouth opened but nothing came out.

The woman stopped at a reception desk. He followed and looked at the woman behind the counter.

"Hello, Jason." She smiled. "Quentin is expecting you. I'm Jane, his secretary. If you ever need anything, just ask. Please go in." She got up and opened a door next to her desk. Jason walked in and noticed a man sat behind a desk working on some papers.

He glanced up and went back to his papers on his desk as if Jason was insignificant. His secretary closed the door behind Jason. He looked around the room. A large American flag was on the back wall. Other walls had pictures of old aircraft, mostly black and white pictures. One picture caught Jason's eye. It was Quentin Roosevelt Military Academy, the American school he had attend a year earlier.

"Sit down boy," the man said. Immediately, Jason could tell he was American. Jason sat in front of the man's desk and said nothing. The old man looked up and came around to meet him. Jason noticed he was in a wheelchair. The old man shook Jason's hand. Jason thought he looked about seventy. He was bald and had a bad scare across the right of his face.

"Hello," Jason said.

"I would love to know what is going through your mind right now?" the old man asked, nodding at Jason.

"Yeah, it would start with who are you and where am I?" Jason said.

"You don't recognize me?" the man asked.

"Oh yeah I got it. Elvis Presley am I right?" Jason said.

The old man wheeled himself back behind his desk. He was clearly annoyed with Jason's remark. "I can see why they suspended the entire academy now."

"Academy? What's that got to do with anything, and why do you have a picture of it on your wall?" Jason asked.

"Let me explain. I'm Quentin Roosevelt. You went to the academy that was named after me. I had hoped you would recognize me from some pictures they have hanging on the walls. You were there for a few months."

"He was killed in World War One and was about twenty, not…." Jason paused, trying not to sound rude. "You are older, give or take sixty years," Jason said.

"Correction, I was shot down over France in July 1918. They never found my body. I was brought back here, barely alive, with no legs and a burnt body, but I can assure you I never died."

"That would make you about…" Jason started.

"Well it's 1976 now so seventy nine."

"Um, yeah. Why didn't you let people know you were alive?"

"America had its fair share of Roosevelts. I could do more here with my family in its place."

The door opened and closed again. Jason turned to see Dexter Delong join them. "Morning, sir. I see you've met him," Dexter said taking a seat next to Jason.

"Yes and the short time you acted as his father you obviously never taught him any manners. Still, that will change." Quentin said.

Jason sat quietly, waiting for an explanation. Eventually, he spoke to Quentin. "Why am I here? Am I in trouble or danger?" His voice broke off. He started to get worried.

Dexter spoke first. "No Jason, you are not in any danger and not in any trouble. We've been watching you for a few years now, ever since the Jakarta massacre. We heard about an eleven-year-old boy who, not only recovered the cassette, but rescued the Marines and flew an aircraft back to Australia and landed it even after being hit by shrapnel. Since then, you were on our radar. We've been trying to find a way to extract you and bring you here."

"Why?" Jason asked.

"I thought it obvious. However, that damn George Young sent you undercover and almost got you killed. Somehow, you survived that, and just when things looked like we could approach your father, you were whisked off to the Academy," Quentin said.

"We were about to make our move, but when your father was held captive by the Vietnamese, you went AWOL and travelled half way around the world to rescue him," Dexter said. "To be honest, we didn't think you would survive that. However, you did, and again when you got back to the UK, George Young sent you undercover to spy on the IRA. You discover it's your uncle and closed that case."

"No, it was Scott that worked it out," Jason said.

"Ah yes, the brilliant Scott Turner, has one of the highest IQ's in Britain. We looked at him too, but he's not got the full package to be a candidate. You do," Quentin said.

"Scott has the full package. He's really clever, he knows more than any teacher at the school, and can work out a puzzle in seconds," Jason said.

"Agreed," Dexter said, placing his hand on Jason's knee. "But he can't fly a plane, kill with his bare hands, take on five or six adults, climb a castle with his bare hands, swim, or run like you. And we didn't get a special request to bring him here like we did you. "

Jason moved his knee away from Dexter's hand. "What special request?"

"Let's just call it a Royal Decree."

"Do you want me to work for the CIA?"

"No Jason, most of the CIA works for us," Quentin said.

"Us?" Jason asked.

"Infinity. We have various agencies working for and with us, such as the American CIA, the British MI6 & SAS, the Russian KGB, the French SDECE, the German BND, Australian ASIO, and so on," Quentin said.

"What do you do?" Jason asked.

"Jason, we do what you do, but on a much larger scale. We train the very best to be the best. Quentin Roosevelt was here as a boy, he became a fighter ace in World War One before he was shot down. Many others have come here, such as a brilliant young man who came here in 1886 aged twelve. By 1895 he was in Cuba acting as a spy for us. 1896 he was in India with the British army. Two years later, he was sent to Sudan and in 1899 to South Africa for the Boar War. Eventually, he was caught and imprisoned. Of course, with the training he had while at Infinity, the prison couldn't hold him and he escaped," Dexter said.

Quentin continued. "I met him here in 1916. He was always close to Infinity, so much so years later we persuaded many to push him into power in Great Britain. Hitler needed to be stopped. We needed to stop him. So, he became Britain's Prime Minister."

Jason's mouth opened wide in amazement. "Do you mean Sir Winston Churchill?"

"Why of course, and with Franklin D Roosevelt as US President, we had what we needed to help us steer victory."

"Wow, have you had other famous people come here?" Jason gasped.

"We currently have two Presidents and a Prime minister, countless foreign secretaries, military commanders. They all started here and learnt the trade," Quentin said. "And we feel you have what it takes to become part of the team."

"I don't want to be a Prime Minister. I

want to join the SAS or MI6," Jason argued.

"We didn't exactly plan on making you Prime Minister, Jason. You don't fit the bill. You are more hands on, much more suited in the field. Yes, The SAS or MI6 are perfect for you. But for now, you are a very valuable commodity. No one suspects a boy. The training Wong Tong gave you is better than we could possibly train you with martial arts. However, you are a lousy shot with a gun, you have not been taught how to defuse a bomb, how to break into a high security building, pick a lock, steal a car without a key, or amputate a limb," Dexter said.

"Amputate a limb?" Jason cringed. "Why would I want to learn how to do that?"

"Imagine you are on a joint mission and someone with you gets badly injured. Can you stitch a wound? Amputate a leg that has gangrene? You need to be trained in all aspects of military first aid."

For over an hour, Jason listened to Quentin and Dexter explain everything. He was to attend the school and do some subjects up in the main school such as math, English, and languages. However, weapons & target practice, bomb making, planting, and defusing lessons will be down here. Other students would also learn martial arts, but no doubt Jason could teach the instructors a thing or two. He would be taught all aspects of military training, parachute landing, and first aid.

At Infinity, all students are elite. They are the most athletic, the most technically advanced, and the smartest and toughest kids in the world. The more he heard, the more he liked it. Until he found a flaw in the plan.

"Does Brenda or my dad know about this?" Jason asked.

"Of course not. George Young didn't and your father does not need to know," Dexter said.

Jason looked disappointed. "I don't think that will work. I made a promise that I won't ever lie to my father."

"It's a white lie Jason. He just needs to know you are okay at this school. He doesn't need to know all the subjects."

Jason paused before answering. "I lied to him once and got spanked, but worse was I disappointed him. I didn't just promise him. I made the promise to myself that I would never lie to him again."

"From the reports I've read on you Jason, I couldn't imagine anyone spanking you."

Quentin smiled.

"He's my dad."

Dexter studied Jason before coming up with a solution. He suggested that Jason be selective with the information he gives his father. This way, he would not have to lie. Jason reluctantly agreed, but it didn't fit well with him. He was unsure what he would tell Scott. So for now, he put it out of his thoughts.

CHAPTER NINETEEN

Jason was shown around by Dexter. It was much larger than he had first imagined. He was given his own room; it shared a bathroom with five other rooms in the boys block. Jason would later meet his fellow students. They were all currently out on a three day hike across Belgrad Forest. The large rugged forest situated just outside Istanbul was often used by Infinity for training purposes. They would be returning later today.

He was shown to his room and told to change into his new uniform. He was surprised to find his suitcase on the bed and his toothbrush and comb laid out in the bathroom for him. His closet contained several uniforms—he same black pants and black top with the Infinity Global logo on the chest. He tried it on and it fit him perfect. He wondered how they knew his exact sizes. His room was fitted with a comfortable bed, TV, and radio.

His first lessons would start the following day. For now, he explored. This was cut short when he found the gym. He stripped to the waist and worked out performing karate katas. He spent the next hour attacking a punch bag with various kicks, punches, and chops.

Jason was so consumed on the bag he never noticed three boys enter. They stood and watched him for a while before coming closer. He punched the bag in rapid succession and finished it off with a roundhouse kick.

"Keeah," he shouted as he gave it a final blow. Sweat trickled down his chest. He brushed his long blond bangs out of his eyes and noticed his audience.

"Hi." Jason panted.

"Whoa! So you're the great Jason Steed we have all heard about. I can't wait to spar with you. I heard you are one of the best martial artists ever to have come here." A boy walked forward. Jason guessed he was around fourteen, Asian, with large rimmed glasses. "I'm Kevin," he said.

The boy took off his shoes and socks as he approached Jason and stood in a fighting stance. Jason was already out of breath but went along with it and matched the stance. Immediately, Kevin stood upright and took a step back.

"This is non-contact right? Just sparring. I want to see if you are as good as they say you are," Kevin said nervously.

"Sure," Jason said.

They faced each other, both balancing on the balls of their feet. Jason concentrated, trying to gauge his opponent. He didn't want to hurt Kevin but didn't want to look foolish either. He figured if Kevin was a student at Infinity, he would be better than average at karate. His thoughts were quickly confirmed.

Kevin stepped forward and tried to sweep Jason's front leg away. Jason lifted it clear and threw out a dummy kick to hold Kevin back. Kevin attacked with a roundhouse kick and switched to a sidekick. Jason stood aside and blocked. He threw a dummy kick again. Kevin had guessed the move and attacked back, narrowly missing Jason's face with his left foot.

The move was too close for comfort. Jason leapt forward, spun, and threw a roundhouse kick at Kevin. "Keeah," Jason shouted.

He pulled his kick. His foot just touched Kevin's ribs, but it was enough to knock him back a few feet. Kevin stood back and bowed. "Wow, you're fast. Good point. You have to teach me that move." Kevin smiled. He walked forward and shook Jason's hand.

The second boy was younger. Jason thought he looked around twelve. He spoke with a German accent and called himself Karl. He took of his shoes and socks, followed by his shirt. Jason was surprised how well built he was for his age. His body was slender and muscles well defined, much like his own body.

"Can I try?" Karl asked.

Jason nodded and stood in a fighting stance. As soon as Karl stood in the same position. Jason moved forward fast. Before Karl could do anything, Jason had swept his legs from under him. Karl fell to the ground, and immediately, Jason pounced on him, pinning him down. He pulled his right arm back and struck stopping an inch from Karl's nose. Karl's eyes almost popped out of his head.

"Holy smokes," Karl said. "That was

pretty scary."

Jason smiled and lifted his sweating body off of Karl. He lifted Karl up from the ground.

"Thanks, Jason. It was an honor to get my butt kicked by you," Karl said.

"Really?" Jason asked.

"You are just thirteen and you have already been shot at and killed people. You don't know how lucky you are! Not many of us have been on real missions yet, just the older students," Karl said, almost bowing.

The third youth introduced himself as Connor. He was fourteen and from New Zealand. He removed his shirt, revealing a stocky and very muscular physique. Jason had never seen someone so young with such a well-developed body. "Good day, mate," Connor said.

"Hi Connor, nice to meet you. Australian?" Jason asked.

"No mate, I'm from the land of the 'All Blacks,'" Connor said.

Jason thought for a second. He wasn't into any sports apart from martial arts, but the 'All Blacks' were the world's greatest Rugby team.

"Oh, New Zealand. Cool."

"So Jason, you think you could do that to an *All Black*?" Connor asked.

"You're not an *All Black* Connor," Kevin said.

"Not yet, but my dad was and my older brother Vic plays for them," Connor argued.

"Do you do karate as well?" Jason asked.

"Nah mate, Judo and rugby are my sport," Connor said. "They say you have a black belt in judo as well as karate, is that right?"

"Yes," Jason said.

"Think you could stop me?" Connor asked.

"Sure."

"I bet I could pin you up against that wall," Connor said, pointing at the wall that was some twenty feet behind Jason.

"No way, Connor. He will kick your arse," Karl said.

"Try it." Jason smiled.

Connor ran forward towards Jason as fast as he could. Jason blocked Connors right hand, but Connor's left hand wrapped around Jason waist. He picked up Jason, spun him almost upside down, and kept running. For several strides, Jason struggled in vain. Connor was rapidly approaching the wall at an alarming speed, and it was clear Jason was going to be used as his cushion.

Jason's right arm was hooked over Connors head, unable to do anything. His legs were almost on Connors shoulders. Jason had his left hand free and was left with only one option. He grabbed Connors private parts and squeezed. For a few steps, Connor ignored the pain and kept going forward, his powerful legs striding towards the wall. Jason's weight was nothing to him, so Jason squeezed as hard as he could.

"Agh! let go," Connor screamed, falling to his knees. He dropped Jason, who wrapped his legs around Connor's neck and twisted, throwing Connor onto his back. Using all of his strength, Jason held him in a headlock until Connor submitted.

"That was cheating! You grabbed my meat and two veg," Connor complained.

"I knew you wouldn't be able to pin him against the wall," Kevin laughed.

"He cheated and grabbed my package," Connor complained, rubbing his private parts. "Steed, you cheated."

"Come on, don't make such a fuss over such a *little* thing," Jason joked, wriggling his little finger at Connor.

Kevin and Karl roared with laughter. Connors pride was hurt. He glared at Jason. He started to walk away, still holding his private parts.

Jason walked towards him. "Hey sorry, Connor, no hard feelings? I had to do something, mate, you was gonna crush me against the wall," Jason said, holding out a hand of friendship.

Connor stopped and smiled at Jason and shook his hand. "Okay, but you ever touch me there again and I'll..." He was interrupted before he could finish.

"Believe me mate, it's the last place on Earth I want to put my hand again," Jason said. "How many other students are here?"

"Fourteen with you." Kevin nodded towards Jason. "Us three, seven girls, and three older boys, all sixteen."

"Oh, I thought there would be more,"

Jason said.

"We generally hang out together and keep Connor out of trouble," Karl said. "It'll be cool if you want to hang with us as well."

Jason smiled and looked at Connor for approval. He thought Connor seemed to be the one in charge. Connor grinned and nodded. The boys spent the evening together bringing Jason up to speed on everything.

He discovered it wasn't very often that someone new joined them at Infinity. They had all been told in advance Jason was coming and his accomplishments. Not even the older boys had done anything as daring as Jason. Mostly, they were planted to find out information, act as lookouts. The most common use for them was to access secure buildings, posing as teenage thugs who broke in looking for cash. The real objective was secret information that could be used by Infinity on criminal organizations or terrorists.

To make it look more like a random break-in, they often took tins of spray paint and painted graffiti on the walls. Often breaking in at weekends and copying the secrets they needed. On Monday, the staff would notice the break-in and graffiti and assume it was just kids. They would never check to see if secret files had been tampered with.

The other advantage was, should they ever get caught, they could use the same story until a member of Infinity could get them released. Infinity had so many contacts with various law enforcement agencies and government secret services that any member of Infinity would not be held for very long.

Karl, Connor, Kevin, and Jason sat in Jason's room on the floor eating peanuts, mostly by flicking them in the air and catching them in their mouths. They told Jason their own special abilities. Karl explained he could hold his breath for nearly fifteen minutes. He also was a brilliant swimmer and top marksman. He was a member of the German army cadets. His record scores as a marksman and his ability to hold his breath under water were noticed by Infinity so he was recruited.

Kevin was from South Korea. His teachers suspected he was a boy genius but further investigation found he had a photographic memory. He could read any schoolbook and remember all the answers. Infinity use him for gathering information. He was also a black belt in Taekwondo and was studying for his Second Dan. He was one of the youngest in South Korea to achieve black belt at age eight.

Connor came from a sporting family. He won the New Zealand junior weighting competition at age ten, beating many fourteen–year-olds. He held a black belt in Judo, plays for the Junior All-Blacks Rugby team when he is home, and can run a hundred meters in eleven seconds. His burst of speed and power for a young boy made him a perfect candidate for Infinity.

Jason learnt from his new friends how some of the girls could climb a sheer rock face, a twenty-five story building. They made excellent cat burglars. All the students had a great natural gift that gave them an ability to do the unexpected. In espionage, using a child no one would suspect was a useful tool that Infinity had been utilizing for decades.

At five am, the early morning buzzer went off. Jason had been instructed the day before. He slipped on his jogging pants, shirt, and shoes and ran to the main hall. He met up with Karl and Kevin, as most of the other students arrived. Jason pulled his long bangs over his eyes. Everyone was looking at him, being he was the new student.

"Where's Connor?" Jason asked Kevin.

"He's always the last one here," Kevin said. No sooner had he said it and they heard someone break wind loudly behind them. Most of the students complained. Jason turned and saw Connor walking towards him waving his hands at his back-side.

"Oh that one's gonna be ripe mate, all those peanuts we ate." Connor laughed. Kevin, Karl, and Jason all sniggered.

A girl who Jason guessed she was about fifteen glared at the boys. "That's all we need, another gross immature boy. I thought you were more grown-up Jason. There is nothing funny about Connor. He is disgusting," she said. Jason thought she sounded American.

"It was just a fart. We all do it, even stuck up Canadians like you," Connor said. The girl raised her nose in the air and strode off. Connor turned to Jason. "Don't take no notice of Mosquito Bites, she thinks her poop doesn't stink."

"Mosquito Bites?" Jason asked, not knowing why she was given that nickname.

"Yeah did you see her chest?" Connor laughed.

"No," Jason said.

"Exactly. I've seen bigger mosquito bites,"

Connor said.

Jason roared with laughter. He knew it was wrong to tease someone, but the casual way Connor mentioned it in his Australian accent made it all the more amusing. Jason took an instant liking to Connor and was already feeling comfortable with his new school.

The large door opened and the students followed the corridor. It went back up to the school room 1G. They all made their way out onto the school running track. Waiting for them was a well-built man in his late forties wearing a black tracksuit with the Infinity logo. Jason suspected he was ex-military with the way he carried himself. He walked with his chest un-naturally sticking out. He has a baldhead. Jason couldn't work out if he had lost his hair or shaved his head.

"Okay, for the sake of our new recruit, Mr. Jason Steed, I want twelve laps, and anyone I think is slacking will do twenty laps." He paused and looked at the group of youths, many still yawning, some with hair un-brushed and sleep still in their eyes. "Go," he barked.

Jason followed the others and kept with Karl, Kevin, and Connor. He stayed a few paces ahead of Connor. He didn't want to be behind him if he still had gas and be in the direct firing line.

The pace was much faster than he had expected. By the tenth lap he had to push himself to keep with the others to complete the last two laps. When the run was over, they had to perform push-ups, sit-ups, and finish with what they called a warm-down lap of the field.

By six thirty, they all left the school field and returned downstairs. To anyone arriving at the school after six thirty in the morning, there was no evidence that the school track and field had just been used. Infinity kept the fourteen students hidden as they had done for decades.

The students showered and ate breakfast. By nine, they had some lessons upstairs in the main school. Here, they would mingle and make regular friends with the international students. However, for certain lessons, they would go back downstairs to perform lessons in subjects normal school children would never do.

Jason's third lesson was gun practice. He was a novice with a gun but the only one in the class who had actually shot someone before. Karl was by far the best shot in the class of fourteen but was interested in knowing what it was like to shoot someone.

When the lesson was over, Jason turned in

his goggles and ear protection. He threw his paper target in the trash. He had hit it just three times out of thirty shots. Karl, on the other hand, had drawn a smiley face on his paper target with bullets and had his target at one hundred feet compared to everyone else who had targets set at between twenty five to fifty feet.

At lunch, Karl, Kevin, Connor, and Jason sat together in the canteen upstairs in the main school.

"Jason, how many have you killed with a gun?" Karl asked.

"Shush, keep your voice down," Kevin hissed.

"How many Jason, what was it like?" Karl asked again quietly.

Jason tried ignoring the question, but after he repeated it, he finished his mouthful and suddenly looked very serious. "The first person was with a knife. I have also used a gun, a grenade, and once my fist; the impact also broke two of my fingers. Killing someone does not make you feel sad or happy. You feel empty and very ashamed."

The others looked wide-eyed at each other. It was Connor who spoke first. "You killed someone with your fist, just a punch?"

"I hope you never have to, but it was a situation where a friend was killed in front of me. I had no weapon, just my hands. I was told by my karate master never to use the punch until I'm at least sixteen because my bones are not fully developed. However, I had no choice," Jason said glumly.

"What gun were you using when you shot someone? Does their brains splat out everywhere?" Karl asked.

"I don't know much about guns. When you shoot someone or you see someone get shot and the person's eyes are looking at you one second and turn lifeless the next, it's not something you wish to remember or talk about."

"Do you get nightmares?" Connor asked.

Jason signed he wasn't comfortable with the questions. "For those who I hurt or killed, no, it was they or I. But I still see someone who died in my arms almost two years ago, my friend Todd Johnson. We were both eleven, and he was shot." Jason eyes glazed over.

"Hey enough of this," Kevin said. "This is no way to treat our new friend. I'm sure he would rather talk about girls. Did you see any you like

Jason?"

Jason cleared his throat and wiped his eyes. "I never got a chance to see much of them yet. Do you guys have girlfriends?" He smiled and nodded thankfully at Kevin for changing the subject. Kevin smiled back and nodded, his dark Asian eyes watchful and warm. Kevin was the smallest of the group but seemed the most mature.

"Nah, I don't yet, but I have made out with one. Most of the Infinity girls think they are too good for us, and it's hard to date the girls up here because they may ask questions," Connor said.

"Questions?" Jason asked.

"What he means is, you can't get too close to the international students. What if they ask why they only see you for certain lessons or where you live? Then you would have to lie. Not much of a friendship is it?" Kevin said.

"Tim is a sixteen-year-old student who is downstairs with us and Infinity. He goes out with a student up here. He has to be very careful what he says and admits he hates lying to her," Karl said.

*

The afternoon's lesson comprised of military first aid and a class on picking locks. Jason never thought he would ever find a school that he would enjoy. The truth was, he loved it at Infinity. He slowly became a good shot, was able to pick most locks, and became efficient in first aid. Martial arts were good exercise for him. For the most part of the lessons, he showed off his moves and enjoyed sparing with the other students.

He had put off calling his father. He was concerned he may have to lie to him. Although rather than Jason do most of the talking, his father did. He informed Jason that the traffic was getting so bad in London that it made sense for Brenda to stay at the house on a more permanent basis.

The call lasted over ten minutes. Once it was over, Jason realized that he hadn't been asked much. The call was very one sided. It struck Jason that his father had become very close to Brenda and seemed to sound more alive, even younger. It was nice for him to know his father was happy, and if Brenda made him happy then he would just accept her into the family as well. His mother had been dead now since his birth thirteen years ago. It was time his father found someone who he could care for and would love him back.

Scott Turner wasn't so easy to talk to. He

had far too many questions for Jason. On the third attempt to change the subject, Scott stopped him and asked him what was wrong. Jason told him he couldn't say anything over the phone and Scott accepted that. He was far too smart to be lied to, and he was one of the only people in the world apart from his father who he trusted, so he would never lie to him. That made it hard to answer Scott's questions. Jason never called Catherine. He sent her a letter.

CHAPTER TWENTY

The days turned to weeks and the weeks to months Jason wasn't sure how he felt about the prospect of taking six weeks off for recess. He wanted to get home to see his father, Scott, and Catherine. On the other hand he loved the school. He had never been as fit as he was. The morning run and long workouts suited him. He had become close friends with Conner and was amazed by his strength and will power. Conner could bench press two hundred and thirty pounds. For a fourteen-year-old, that was incredible.

An announcement over the speaker system called both Connor and Jason to report immediately to Quentin Roosevelt's office. Both boys ran down the corridor pushing each other into the walls on the way to try and get ahead, even attempting to trip each other up and both laughing. They were still both giggling when they called to go into his office. Dexter sat at the large conference table next to Quentin, along with a female student. It was the Canadian girl who Conner called Mosquito Bites.

"Something amusing Conner?" Dexter asked.

"No sir, we raced here, and he tried cheating pushing me into the wall." Conner grinned.

"That's a lie. I would have beat you here but you kept bumping into me and holding me back." Jason laughed, bumping Connor with his shoulder.

"Well it's good you two get on well. Do you know Cameron?" Dexter asked.

"Yes sir," Both boys answered together.

"Cameron, how well do you know Connor and Jason?" Dexter asked.

She looked at the boys and turned her nose up at them both. "Connor is crude, loud, smelly, and immature. As for Jason, we all heard what a superstar agent he was before he got here, but he seems to follow Conner around laughing at his stupid jokes. I'm surprised Jason isn't more mature."

"Who are you calling smelly, you stuck up b…" Connor stopped himself. "Stuck up Canadian."

"I'm thirteen not thirty. So what if I laugh at Connor's jokes? Some are really funny, especially what he calls you," Jason snapped back.

"Oh yeah, what does he call me?" Cameron cursed, climbing from her seat.

Quentin started laughing and applauded. All three students stopped arguing and looked at him. "Perfect Dexter, just perfect. They will be ideal." He smiled.

"Um, really?" Dexter asked, looking puzzled.

"Of course, have you ever met three teenage siblings that don't fight and argue like that?" Quentin said.

Dexter stood up from his chair and

walked over to the light switches. He flicked them off and turned on a projector. An image of a man in his forties climbing out of a car surrounded by four men in dark suits came on the screen. Dexter used a sword he took from the wall and pointed at the image with his other hand on his hip. He posed as if he was in a sword fight.

"This is William Weinstein. He lives here in Turkey part of the year. He also has homes in Switzerland, America, and Moscow. He was born in Leningrad, Russia and is probably the world's largest underground arms dealers—" Dexter was interrupted.

"That's strange, I thought it was Jason Steed's uncle who was the biggest arms dealer." Cameron sniggered. Jason gave her a dirty look and looked away again.

"No Stuart Steed is one of many smaller dealers who buys from Weinstein and sells directly to military terrorists like the IRA. Weinstein supplies countless dealers like Steed, many to South American rebels, drug cartels, African rebels, and many in the Middle East. Basically anyone who wants to start a war and over throw a government, they would get weapons from a supplier like Stuart Steed, and he would get them from Weinstein," Dexter explained

"Can we stop using my uncle's names in this conversation?" Jason asked, feeling embarrassed.

"If you say so, Jason. But it's not our fault, most have us have a family tree, you must have a cactus…. Because everyone's a prick." Cameron sniggered.

"You can't argue with an *idiot*. She will drag me down to her level and beat me because she has so much experience," Jason snapped back. "Can we leave my family out of this?"

"Yes of course," Dexter said hiding a smirk. "We have reason to believe Weinstein will be staying at a castle in Bodrum here in Turkey for three weeks. We can't be certain but we have the information from a good source. If it's true, his twin children will be with him, both age fourteen, called Ela and Fahad. Ela likes clothes shopping and pop music, and Fahad likes sports, mostly Rugby and martial arts. Both children are given private tuition, but have be known to mix with local children the same age."

"We will be sending you three to Bodrum. I will be going as your father. Your mission is to get to know Ela and Fahad and find out the whereabouts of Weinstein. Cameron, we know you love to shop. Connor is probably better than anyone his age at Rugby, and Jason is to martial arts what the bible is to religion."

All three sat quietly for a while, before Jason spoke. "We sound different. I'm English and speak with an English accent. Connor sounds Australian, and Cameron sounds American."

"I don't sound Aussie. My accent is from New Zealand," Connor argued.

"And I don't sound American. I sound Canadian," Cameron said.

"To anyone else, you three all speak English with an accent from here or there. To Ela and Fahad, you will sound just like you have travelled around from school to school because your father works around the world, just like their father has," Dexter said.

"As I'm the oldest, I take it I'm in charge," Cameron said.

"Ha, no way. What skills have you got apart from being able to parade out like a model?" Connor said. "And not a good model at that."

"I've been on two missions, and I'm the fastest lock picker and pick pocket at Infinity," Cameron snapped back.

"That's nothing to what Jason has done. He should be in charge," Connor said.

Jason said nothing. He was amused by the pair arguing. He watched Quinton's expression, who remained quiet, his watchful eyes absorbing information.

Dexter sighed. "No one is in charge but me. Connor, this is your first mission. You can learn from Cameron and Jason. All you have to do is act as a normal dysfunctional family. The arguing makes it more real. We leave in the morning. Until then, you tell no one of the upcoming mission. It's top secret."

Connor and Jason went into Istanbul in the afternoon. It was the first time Jason had been out into the city. He was surprised how well Connor knew his way around. Jason found it to be a soup of medieval buildings and poorly built modern construction trying to push and smother the older traditional buildings out of their way. Connor took him through back streets and alleyways, past hidden mosques and churches, thriving market gardens and local bazaars. Jason marveled at the large mosques, with their large domes and massive towers that threatened to spike the clouds that passed overhead.

Connor admitted to Jason he was excited to be finally going on a mission and better still to be going with Jason. He hoped he would have a chance to see Jason in a real fight. Jason took it all in his stride. He was pleased to be going with Connor; he made him laugh. He wasn't sure what to think of Mosquito Bites. She did seem to think she was better than everyone else. Jason told himself it must be because she was older.

CHAPTER TWENTY ONE

The next morning, they met with Dexter, and a car picked them up. From there, it drove them to Bodrum. The journey took just over fourteen hours. Cameron constantly complained about the heat and how much Connor was sweating. Dexter sat up front with the driver. The three students had to sit in the back. Eventually, Cameron swapped with Jason just so she would stop complaining about Connors sweat. Connor was not overweight, but he was stocky. His head sat close to his shoulders. At times, depending how he was standing, he looked like he had no neck at all.

As they passed a sign that read Bodrum, Dexter smiled and started talking. He hadn't said no more than two words the entire journey.

"Ah, Bodrum, sun, sea, and history. I've always wanted to visit here," Dexter said. He was right. The city was fresh and different from anything Jason has ever experienced before. The make believe family would live in a small traditional three bedroom, two story, white, sugar-cube home. Or at least that is what Jason nicknamed the houses. He told Dexter that the white houses piles so close to each over around the harbor look like sugar-cubes from a distance. Connor and Jason would share a room that had a large window with a breath taking view of the village and coastline.

Jason thought everything about the city was almost magical. He told Connor it seemed to rain different here and also the sunrise different and sets completely different. After a few days, Jason mentioned it again. He truly loved the city. He told Connor that the wind blows different, sea smells fresh.

Dexter also mentioned that Bodrum is the proudest, the most inert, the most beautiful, the most honest, and almost a modern child of Nature Mother. As well as the modern sugar-cubed homes and shops, ancient Roman buildings and tombs built over three hundred years before Christ himself was born.

The fresh air reminded Jason of the mountains that over looked Hong Kong. He wished he had learned to meditate. He had watched his mentor Wong Tong meditate for hours, breathing in all the goodness the world could provide.

Connor and Jason wasted no time and discovered some excellent swimming areas where local boys would dive off a high cliff in an effort to prove how fearless they were. Jason and Connor both jumped off the thirty-foot cliff into the warm Mediterranean Sea a few times. Cameron spent hours walking through the palm-lined streets, window-shopping and taking pictures of the scenery. She wore a pair of short shorts that barley covered her. She enjoyed the whistles and looks she received from local teenagers and some men.

After just three days, Jason and Connor finally met Fahad when they noticed three boys were drying off after swimming. The three boys stared at Connor and talked among themselves, occasionally looking up at Connor.

"What are they staring at?" Connor asked Jason.

"I'm not sure. Normally, I would recommend we walk away, but we need to start talking to other boys if we are going to find

Fahad," Jason said.

Connor agreed and walked towards the boys. They all looked his age. All three boys had dark hair and large brown eyes. Jason assumed they were all local boys.

"Hi." Connor smiled.

The boys all smiled back and nodded. "What are you guys looking at? Connor asked.

"You American?" one boy with Strabismus eyes asked. "You speak English." The boy's eyes were so badly crossed looking in different directions, Connor wasn't sure if he was talking to him or Jason.

"Something like that. Your English is good," Connor said. "I'm Connor, and this is my little brother Jason. Do you know me? Why are you all looking at me?" Although as soon as Connor asked it, Jason felt bad for the boy. His eyes were so crossed and maybe he wasn't looking at them at all.

The same boy walked forward. "Sorry if you thought we were staring, but we were talking about you. Do you and brother live in a gym? You have bigger muscles than my dad."

Connor clenched his arms and posed. "Yeah, I work out. Do you guys dive off that wall?" Connor asked, pointing at a wall that surrounded a small road that meandered around houses up the hill. Conner and Jason had seen a few jump off it, but they decided it was far too risky and never tried it.

"No that's nuts, but Farah did once," the boy with the cross eyes said, pointing at his friend behind him.

The boy he called Farah walked forward and smiled. "I did it once. No big deal."

Jason and Connor looked at each other. Jason was surprised how easy it had been to find him.

"You're crazy." Connor laughed. "That's much too high., your nuts must have been squashed up your backside."

Farah and his two friends laughed. "Nah, it was nothing," Farah boasted.

"Yeah, I bet you were shaking like a leaf and as white as a sheet when you got out the water afterwards," the cross-eyed boy said.

Jason stepped forward. "We're new here. Our dad is working here for the summer. What do you guys do for fun, apart from swimming?" Jason asked. Jason studied Farah. He was just like the picture Infinity had showed them—thin, dark hair, dark brown eyes, and black eyebrows that met in the middle. Jason noticed he had some hair above his top lip and would probably have to start shaving very soon. He had dark skin that gave him a distinct Middle Eastern appearance.

Farah beamed. "Cool. My dad works here for part of the year as well. I can show you all the places tourists don't get to see but on one condition."

"What condition?" Connor asked, folding his arms together and sticking out his chest.

"So I know you two are not nerds, one of you has to jump off the wall," Farah said, pointing up at the wall.

Connor and Jason looked at each other and up at the wall. "Ha that's easy. Even my little brother Jason could do that," Connor said pointing at Jason.

"What?" Jason said, giving Connor a dirty look.

"Well, you are younger than us so if you want to hang with us, prove you are up to it," Connor said.

"How old are you?" Farah said.

"Same as you fourteen," Connor said.

Jason immediately interrupted. "Connor's good with ages. Is he right, are you fourteen as well?" Jason gave Connor another dirty look. They had read it on the case file, but to keep the story real had to pretend, they didn't know. It was obvious to Jason that Connor wasn't very smart and this type of mistake could prove to be dangerous on a mission.

Farah smiled at Jason. "He's spot on. I'm fourteen. Go on then go up the hill, climb the wall, and jump. Make sure you take a run at it so you can get a good leap. If not, you may hit the rocks at the bottom, and I had my lunch today. I don't want to throw up when I see your skull smash open."

Connor roared with laughter. He was clearly over acting, trying to act tough around Farah. Jason thought he was trying too hard to befriend him.

Jason kicked off his shoes and gave his shirt to Connor. "Hold these please," Jason said in a contemptuous tone and pushed his shirt and shoes into Connors chest, knocking him back.

"What?" Connor asked, trying to act innocent.

Jason followed the narrow road up the hill. He couldn't believe he was going to actually jump. He tried to come up with an excuse. He came to the stone wall and climbed up. The sharp slate bricks scratched his bear toes as he climbed. Once at the top he looked down.

"No bloody way," he said, although no one could hear him. He looked down and saw Connor, Farah, and the other two boys waving at him. A few other people had gathered and looked up as well. Jason stood on the top and looked down as if he was going to actually jump. He looked down. Waves gently slapped over the rocks below. If he was going to jump, Farah was right, he would need to get a good push off to clear them.

He was surprised by the amount of wind. He licked his finger and held it up to check the wind direction. That made him feel worse. It was blowing towards him and would push him back into the wall of rocks. He glanced down and now another four or five people had joined the others and looked up at him. A girl stood next to Farah. From this distance Jason was unsure if it was his twin sister Ela, but she looked the same age.

Jason looked down at the water one more time. He couldn't go through with it. He was sure he could in a life and death situation, but this was ridiculous. He could get killed for nothing. Connor was shouting at him and the others were beckoning him to jump. Jason couldn't hear what

Connor was shouting. He turned to climb down and noticed the girl again. If he wanted to get close to her, this was a good way to impress her.

Jason took a deep breath, steadied himself, and concentrated. He built up an adrenaline rush into his system. If he was going to jump, he would at least try and get a good leap. His pupils dilated back; he could no longer hear the sound of the waves or the gulls flying overhead. He concentrated on the jump.

Connor looked up and was now suddenly concerned that Jason was actually going to jump. "Jason don't. It's too dangerous," Connor shouted.

"Is he really going to jump?" Farah asked.

"I think so. I wish I never said anything now. I didn't think he would actually try." Connor paused. "No, if you did it Farah, I'm sure he will be all right."

"Um. I didn't really do it. I made it up…" Farah stammered.

Jason took one more deep breath. He held himself back like a sprinter on the starting blocks. He leapt forward, took two paces, and leapt out into the air. He jumped, maybe for the last time. He was pleased with the distance he gained. He had managed to jump eight to nine feet away from the wall. He looked down and was still falling, faster and faster. It seemed like an eternity. His feet crashed into the water. It swallowed him whole. He kept going down until his foot hit a rock way down deep. He was twisted and tumbled by the strong current.

I'm alive, he said to himself. *I need air.* He fought with the strong undercurrent to surface. His body tangled in seaweed, back and forth with the current. It was harder than he expected trying to fight his way up to the surface. He calmed himself down and remembered training at Sea Cadets. If you get caught in a rip current, swim with it. He tried going with it and went out deeper. The current was stronger, but soon he hoped to be clear. His lungs burnt for oxygen. A hand caught his forearm and pulled him up. The hand continued to pull him to the surface and eventually the person's other hand slid under his body and pushed him to the surface.

Jason took a welcomed deep breath of air. He cleared his eyes and noticed it was Connor that was holding him.

"You okay?" Connor asked.

"Yeah," Jason gasped.

"You're bloody stupid. I didn't think you

would really do it mate," Connor snapped. "Whatever did you really do that for? I thought you was a gonna. If I could, I would kick the stuffing out of you."

Farah gasped a sigh of relief when he saw Jason's distinguishably blond hair break the water's surface.

Both boys swam back to the beach. Jason was given an applause. Farah came to meet them. He passed Jason his shirt and shoes. "You're crazy Jason," Farah said.

Jason turned to Connor. "Thanks. I was having trouble in the current."

"That's what big brothers are for," Connor said, threatening him with his fist. "But you do something so reckless again and I will break your nose."

"No, a decent big brother would never let his younger brother do something so stupid. He could have been killed," The girl who stood next to Farah said.

Jason looked at her. He recognized her from the photos he had seen in the case file. However she looked much better looking in real life. She had long dark hair, large brown eyes, and dark olive skin. Jason thought she could be a model. "I'm fine. Hi, I'm Jason," he said.

"Hello Jason. I'm Farah's sister, Ela."

"Hi I'm Connor. You look alike, are you twins?" Connor said almost, knocking Jason out of the way as he moved forward to shake her hand.

"Yes, we are," Ela said.

"I know this is forward of me, but I have to tell you Ela, if you were a bogey, I would pick you first," Connor said.

"What?" Ela gasped.

"Eeewwwwwww Connor that's the worst chat up line I have ever heard," Jason said. "Sorry Ela. We all have a black sheep in the family, and you just met ours."

"Shut it, Jason. Ela did you just fart? Because you just blew me away," Connor said.

Everyone burst out laughing except Connor. He looked hurt. While Jason dressed, someone suggested they get a drink. As they walked towards, a café Jason took Connor to one side.

"Hey mate, your chat up lines may work in Australia with Aussie girls, but here they sound terrible. You sound like an idiot." Jason said.

"I'm not bloody Australian. I'm from New Zealand. You fancy her, don't you? Well I saw her first," Connor argued.

"She likes me not you. You work on Farah as a good friend since you're both *fourteen*," Jason said.

"Yeah, sorry about that. It sort of slipped out, but now you've proven yourself to Farah, you could be his friend, and I will work my magic on Ela," Connor said.

"You don't have magic when it comes to girls, if you are going to talk about bogeys and farts." Jason laughed.

The Lokanta café was built into the mountain. It had been a café for over two hundred years. Local men at a table at the far end sat and smoked on Hookah's. The sight of them fascinated Jason and Connor who called them water pipes but Farah corrected them. The men passed the mouthpiece to one another and blew out smoke as they exhaled.

Some tourist sat at the center tables drinking local wines. Farah, Ela, Jason, Connor, and one remaining friend of Farah's sat towards the front. Jason wasn't sure what happened to the boy with cross-eyes. Another group of teenagers sat at the next table. Jason guessed this is where the young people would meet up.

They ordered Cokes and said hello to other diners at the café. Ela explained that regulars always greet anyone who comes to the cafe since they believe friendships made here last forever. Jason was sat next to Ela, although when he went to use the rest room, he found Connor in his seat trying to get close to her. As much as Connor tried, he couldn't compete with Jason's gorgeous looks. His Sapphire blue eyes, lightly tanned face, and blond bangs that fell over his eyes made him adorable.

Jason smiled at her when he came back. "Is Connor annoying you?" he asked and flashed his smile again, gently brushing his bangs away from his eyes with a little finger in a move that was purposely slow.

"No, he has stopped with the crazy chat up lines." Ela laughed.

"I'll have you know, most girls love my charm," Connor said.

Farah leant over the table and looked at Connor. "You sound Australian, and Jason sounds more like a Brit."

"Yes, I thought the same," Ela said.

"Um. Do we?" Connor said nervously, looking at Jason for help.

"I wouldn't be surprised if we didn't sound, French, German, Spanish, and Japanese as well. We have moved around so much and gone to so many schools. Connor mixes with guys in his class, and I do with my own age," Jason said, covering the question. "You don't exactly sound Turkish; Farah and Ela sounds slightly European."

Jason wasn't sure if Farah was suspicious or if he was paranoid, but he thought he had covered the answer well enough.

After a few hours, they went their separate way after agreeing to meet up tomorrow to explore Bodrum castle. Farah said people who built it back in the 15th Century haunted it. Jason thought it sounded boring but agreed. It was a way to stay close to Farah and Ela, which was the mission objective. Plus, he liked Ela, so that helped with the objective.

Jason and Connor walked back to the apartment together. Both kept quiet until Connor eventually broke the silence.

"Jason, I think our best plan is to let me

go for Ela. She is my age and she likes me. I know you like her but you're too young for her. If not we may fight over her and that could damage the mission," Connor said.

"Bull. She is only one year older than me, and *she likes* me. You made a fool of yourself with your stupid chat up lines. I can get close to her, and you and Farah can hang out," Jason argued.

"If we can't agree we will let Dexter decided when we have a debrief tonight," Connor said as a matter of fact.

"Debrief?" Jason asked.

"Yeah mate on an Infinity mission they debrief us every day and make notes. This gets reported back to Infinity, and they assess us to make sure we are making progress. It's in the Infinity handbook and part of our lessons. You just haven't been with us long enough to know. Like I said, it would be better that I stick close to Ela."

"You're right. I haven't been in the class as long as you, reading handbooks. I have been on real missions and don't make stupid mistakes like knowing Farah's age," Jason argued. Connor stopped in his tracks and looked serious for once.

"Yeah, I would prefer it if you never

mentioned that. It kind of slipped out," Connor meekly said.

"I won't say nothing but." Jason paused his attention was drawn to a building behind Connor. "Whoa look at that." Jason ran over to the building Connor followed.

Jason looked wide-eyed up at a sign above the building. It read "Sayokan" in large black letters on a red sign.

"Sayokan, what's that? The way you said Whoa, I was expecting to see a naked girl or something," Connor asked.

"I forgot Turkey had its own form of martial arts. It's called Sayokan, It's rare, only a few practice it," Jason said walking into the building. Jason kicked off his shoes inside and bowed before entering. He was noticed by a man sat at a table in the far corner looking at papers. Connor followed and did the same as Jason.

The man stood and came around his desk and bowed. Jason bowed back. "Do you speak English, sir?" Jason asked.

"Hiç İngilizce," the man replied.

"Me Sayokan?" Jason asked, pointing at himself.

The man understood. He spoke back in Turkish but it was clear Jason and Connor couldn't understand. He pointed at the clock at the number six, and then on the calendar, he pointed at tomorrow's date.

"Tomorrow six o'clock. Okay, how much?" Jason asked waving a few Turkish lira at him.

The man nodded and said "Iki" and held two fingers up. Jason thanked him, bowed, and left, dragging Connor with him.

"You look like you just won the lotto," Connor laughed. "You're not seriously going to go tomorrow to learn Turkish Martial arts? I thought you already had about twenty black belts in various forms."

"No, we are. I have three black belts, two of them are third Dan. Only three styles and Judo of course. I may learn something and you will," Jason said.

"We're on a mission, not training," Connor said.

"We have to stay fit, and besides, if I can learn something new I will. It will do you good. Martial arts frees the mind and keeps you alive."

"Yeah well, if you jump off a wall like you

did today and get swallowed up by the sea again, all the martial arts in China won't save you."

The debriefing took an hour with both Connor and Jason. Dexter wanted to know everything. Both boys never mentioned Connor's slip up, but both gave concerns regarding Ela. It was clear they both liked her and neither wanted that to jeopardize the mission. Dexter told them he would think on it.

Just after nine thirty, both boys climbed into their beds. Dexter knocked at the door and walked in. Both boys glared at him.

"Why bother knocking?" Connor said. "I bet you don't just barge into Mosquito Bites' room like that. Talking about her, what did she do today? Go shopping? Paint her nails?"

"Actually, Cameron was taking pictures all day. She pretended to be taking pictures of Bodrum, but she got many of our target, and she met him today. We are all boys together. Don't be so sensitive," Dexter said, sitting on the bottom of Connors bed before continuing.

"I have been thinking about the Ela situation. You have both complicated things. You are supposed to just make friends with the twins. However, this could be an advantage, and I think it's wrong for me to choose. If we truly want to get her trust that could lead to information, then let nature fight it out."

"Gladly." Jason smiled.

Connor looked horrified.

"No. Not literally fight, Jason. Just let nature take its course. If she prefers one of you over the other, she will make her thoughts clear," Dexter said.

"You're not so tough, Steed. I saved your life today," Connor said.

"No, you just helped me. I would have got out eventually," Jason said.

"Good point, Connor. Jason, that was pretty damn reckless. Don't do that again. We pride ourselves on keeping our teen agents alive. It's not very often we lose one. Even during the Second World War we never lost an agent. To lose one on an act of stupidity would be a shame," Dexter said.

Jason sucked his lips together before giving a tight-lipped smile. "Sorry."

"Accepted. Now, you boys get to sleep. You both need your beauty sleep if you are going to woo Ela."

"Connor would need to sleep for a year." Jason laughed.

"You would need to sleep for ten years just to catch up with me," Connor said, throwing his pillow at Jason. Dexter folded his arms and looked serious again.

"Jason, the Turkish karate is a no go. If you went, you could bring attention to yourself," Dexter said.

"What! That's stupid." Jason cursed and leapt from his bed. "Why not? Am I supposed to just hang around and do nothing? I haven't done Sayokan before. I'll be a novice. That won't bring any attention."

"Where martial arts are concerned, Jason, you are no way a novice. That's my decision you can practice karate with Connor in the back yard."

"But I can learn something new. I won't hurt anyone or expose myself," Jason whined before Connor interrupted.

"Eeewwww don't expose yourself, Jason, that's disgusting." Connor laughed.

Jason turned to Connor. "I didn't mean exposing myself like that."

Connor laughed at Jason but quickly stopped when Jason glared at him. "It was just a joke," Connor said.

Dexter walked out and left the two boys arguing. Jason chased after him into the hallway.

"Dexter, I told the guy at the Sayokan studio I would be going tomorrow. I won't blow my cover," Jason argued.

"Ugh put some clothes on," Cameron tutted when she noticed Jason in the hallway wearing just his boxer shorts. She was eating a packet of chips, picking them out with her fingertips.

Dexter swung around and strode purposely towards Jason. "That's my final word on it. I don't want to hear another word about Sayokan. Get to bed." Dexter pointed towards Jason and Connor's bedroom.

Jason stood still for a few moments, thinking what he should do next. Cameron tilted her head and smirked at him before popping another potato chip into her mouth. That made him angrier. Dexter stared at Jason, his finger on his outstretched arm still pointing towards the bedroom. Jason thought back. His uncle Stewart had always told him to obey orders. However, now his uncle no longer had Jason's full respect.

Jason was unsure what to do. He didn't want to back down, but he enjoyed being at Infinity.

"Well, what is it to be?" Dexter asked.

Jason reluctantly nodded. "Yes, sir. Sorry, I'll forget about Sayokan karate." He plodded back into his bedroom and closed the door behind him. Connor watched him climb into bed.

"Jase mate, we can do karate in the back yard if it means that much to you. I may not be as bloody good as you, but I still have a black belt in Judo. So does Mosquito Bites," Connor said.

"Yeah fine, thanks," Jason said, pulling the cover over himself. He wasn't happy with Dexter's rule but figured it was best he did as he was told.

CHAPTER TWENTY TWO

The next two weeks passed by faster than they could have imagined. Connor kept his promise and worked out with Jason most evenings, performing karate katas and Judo holds. Jason found it better than he expected. Connor's strength made him a tough opponent for Judo. Although, when Jason was in trouble and held in a lock he couldn't get out of, he would switch to karate and punch or kick Connor out of the way.

The two of them could be heard grunting one moment, cursing at each other the next, followed by giggles and laughs the next moment.

Cameron had got closer to William Weinstein. She told him she was a student vacationing with her family and was taking photographs of Bodrum for a book she wanted to publish. Weinstein was interested in buying more property, so he employed her to take hundreds of pictures of various buildings in the city. She had been seeing him most days with her results.

Both Connor and Jason were invited by Farah and Ela to their father, William Weinstein's, birthday party. Jason was getting closer to Ela, but as things started to get to the holding hands stage, he stated to get second thoughts.

*

The party was being held at Weinstein's home, a large, old castle that was converted into a luxury home where Farah, Ela, and their father stayed for the summers. The castle was built into the top of a steep rock face that swept steeply down to the sea. At sea level, it had a small private jetty and a small cave. The Weinsteins used it to dock their boats.

Jason and Connor wore a shirt and tie, It was a great evening. They declined a taxi ride from Dexter and walked.

"I guess you won with Ela, mate. She really seems into you," Connor said with his head down and hands in his pockets.

"I need to talk to you about that. I need to pull back and let you get closer to her," Jason said. He lifted his hand up to his chest and felt the silver cross Catherine had given him through his shirt.

"Why mate, lost your bottle?" Connor asked.

"No, I like her," Jason said before pausing, fiddling with his cross. "I guess I like all girls, but I kinda have a girlfriend and feel guilty getting close to other girls."

"Girlfriend, really? Who?"

"In my real life, I have a best friend called Scott and a girlfriend, she is called Catherine," Jason said. He smiled when he thought about Scott and Catherine.

"Catherine, that's a nice name. What's her full name?"

"Um. Well she doesn't really have one."

"Of course she does. We all have a surname. For now on this mission you are Jason Delong. I read your file. On your last missions you have used the name Jason Norris, but you are really called Jason Steed."

"Yeah, but Catherine doesn't use a surname," Jason said.

"Is she that ugly you don't want me to know? I thought we were friends," Connor asked.

"Another ugly remark about Catherine and you'll be going to the dentist tomorrow." Jason grinned. "I think they sometimes use the name Windsor."

Connor stopped in his tracks and caught Jason by his arm. He had a huge grin on his face. "Are you giving me bull? Are you joking or what? You mean Princess Catherine? No way."

"Shush, keep your voice down."

"Seriously, you and her go on dates and stuff?" Connor asked.

"It's not easy. She has a body guard, and in public she has to wear a hat and glasses to hide her face, but yeah," Jason said.

"Oh so now you feel guilty all of a sudden and want Connor to bring on my chick pulling skills and save the mission?" Connor laughed.

"Something like that. But you need to understand, if you get close to Ela, when this mission is over, you won't see her again. It's not easy doing that," Jason said.

"Sure, I can handle that," Connor said.

*

The castle was decorated in flowers and brightly colored sheets that hung from the exterior walls. Guests were greeted at the main door by two butlers dressed in traditional Turkish guard uniforms. Connor said they looked like they were wearing nightshirts with slippers on. Jason burst out with laughter when he looked for himself. Whey wore the royal guard uniform and had fluffy balls of wool on the toes of each shoe.

Connor told him the British Palace Guard looked just as stupid with bear skin hats on. Jason wasn't sure what the dress code was for New Zealand guards to get back at Connor, so he settled with thumping Connor in the arm instead.

The inside of the castle was decorated for the party. One long table was covered with dishes of fresh strawberries. In the center was a huge model of a strawberry that stood nearly six foot. It was made from literally hundreds of strawberries that had been carefully pinned together.

Another table had a fountain of champagne, another had a fountain of chocolate. Some guests held strawberries under the chocolate and covered them in the sweet brown molten liquid.

Around the large dance room, several of the guards in traditional costume stood upright with their hands behind their backs. Jason noticed all of them carried a Turkish sword. He had been told they were called a Kilij. At first, he assumed it was part of the uniform, but as he walked close to one, he noticed it was very real and long. He was unsure why the guards all needed to be armed.

Cameron was already mixing with other guests. She wore a long tight fitting scarlet red dress that hung tightly to her slim body. The dress had a slit up the side that ran up just below her underwear line. Both Connor and Jason's mouths dropped when they saw her.

"Holy cow you look…" Connor said, trying to find the right words. "You are going to start a fire, you look so hot."

"Is that a compliment or is there a crude punch line?" Cameron asked, standing with her hand on her hip.

"A compliment," Connor said.

"Don't try and come onto me. Just the thought of it will make me hurl."

"As much as it hurts me to say it, you look nice Cameron," Jason said.

"Wills has asked me to sit with him during dinner, so I had to make an effort." Cameron smiled.

"Oh it's *Wills* is it? Remember who he is," Connor warned.

"Yeah and remember how old he is. He's old enough to be our father," Jason said.

"You guys know Cameron?" Farah said, walking towards them.

"Yeah she's our sis," Connor said.

Farah looked surprised. "Oh wow what a small world. You never said you knew Connor and Jason," he said to Cameron.

"You never mentioned them. Besides, I try to forget about them." She sneered before walking off.

All three boys watched her walk off. "She's helping my Dad with pictures, although I'm sure he likes her for more than that. He's always got a new girlfriend. They seem to get younger each time," Farah said glumly.

"She's like a cross between an onion and donkey," Farah said.

"Why?" Jason and Connor asked simultaneously.

"Cause she's a piece of ass that will bring a tear to your eye." Farah laughed.

Jason stayed close to Farah. He kept his distance from Ela. He hoped she hadn't noticed his coldness towards her. He gave her one-reply answers. He was nice to her, and slowly she got the message and sat with Connor while they ate dinner.

After dinner, Farah and Jason sat under a parasol at a table, sipping fruit punch out on a sundeck that looked over the Mediterranean Sea and Bodrum. Weinstein's castle was once a monastery. In ancient times, it was used for hiding people from invading armies. Even during World War Two, local Jewish families had used it to seek refuge in its protective walls.

Farah and Jason leant on a brass rail which

surrounded the sundeck looking out at a yacht in the distance. Below, the sea kissed the rock face with each wave. While enjoying the view, they flicked grapes into their mouth, trying to catch them, each time flicking them higher. William Weinstein stepped out onto the sundeck and tried himself. He missed his grape and spilt some of his wine he was holding.

"So Farah, is this the same Jason who dived off the wall?" William Weinstein asked in his strong Russian accent. He placed his hands on the brass rail and deeply inhaled the sea air.

"Yeah he's loco. It's almost as high as this balcony. He's loco with a capital L." Farah laughed.

"Maybe, maybe not. Maybe he is just courageous, and then again, maybe he is foolish. What is it Jason?" William Weinstein asked.

"Um. It was foolish. I was showing off," Jason said.

William Weinstein held out his hand shook and Jason's enthusiastically. "I like the reply. You are honest. My children speak highly of you and your brother. I'm pleased. Tell me Jason, what does your father do?"

"He's an art expert. He looks at really ugly

paintings for people who want him to value them or check they are authentic," Jason said. It was Dexter's undercover job, and Dexter actually did like art. He'd amassed a great knowledge of art and artists. It would be helpful, should anyone ask him a question.

Weinstein nodded and seemed un-interested.

"What do you do, sir?" Jason asked.

Weinstein was taken aback by the question. He popped another grape into his mouth and paused before answering. His eyes narrowed.

"Farah, you tell Jason what your father does for a job," Weinstein asked his son.

"Nude model?" Farah said as if it was a question. "I don't know, you just tell us business."

"Teenage humor, so crude and disrespectful." Weinstein sighed shaking his head disapprovingly. "Business, I buy and sell commodities."

"Stocks and shares?" Jason asked.

"Not quite, a commodity is an item that is needed by someone who is prepared to pay for it.

I buy and sell such items."

Cameron walked out onto the sundeck. Weinstein took her hand and kissed it.

"Dad, did you know Cameron is Jason and Connor's sister?" Farah said.

"No," Weinstein said looking at Cameron and back at Jason. "Your mother must have been very beautiful to have beautiful children like you."

"Dad, you need your eyes tested." Farah laughed.

Weinstein ignored the remark. He was looking down at the ocean and at a small boat that was just off shore getting closer to the rock face. A small landing for boats could just be seen where two men waited for the boat. Cameron looked down at it and watched someone on the boat throw a rope to one of the waiting men. The small boat disappeared into the mountain river out of sight. Then a small speed boat came from inside the mountain estuary and was tied up to the jetty.

"I have to go and take care of some business. I also sell rare wine. That small boat has a buyer interested in a special fine wine I have. Farah, please entertain our guests while I'm gone."

Weinstein marched off. Jason noticed he signaled to one of the guards who followed him.

"I better go and mingle with the other guests while he is busy," Farah said, walking back into the busy dance room. Jason and Cameron looked at each other. Connor joined them.

"Weinstein seems to have taken an interest in you. That seems a little sick. He's old enough to be our dad. You're much too young to be receiving a guest in the cellar," Connor said. Cameron laughed at his remark and blushed. She leant on the waist high concrete wall and looked down at the azure sea, trying to get sight of the small boat that had gone into the opening in the rock face below. Suddenly, someone pushed her and pulled her back.

"Don't," Cameron shrieked.

"I bet that made you jump?" Connor laughed.

"Connor, you are so immature sometimes. What happened, did Ela get tired of your stupid jokes?" Cameron snapped back aggressively.

"No, she is mingling with the guests while her dad takes care of some business. Someone has come to pick up some fancy wine," Connor said.

The three of them chatted on the balcony, enjoying the welcome cooler fresh air that came as the day started to come to an end. Connor and Cameron continued to bicker, much to Jason's amusement.

After fifteen minutes, the boat pulled off and appeared again and slowly set off out to sea.

"Looks like the guy got his bottle of wine," Connor said. "I like the dolphins painted on the side of the boat."

Jason looked and studied it. "That's a different boat."

"No, it's the same one. But I didn't notice the dolphins before either," Cameron said.

Jason looked again at the blue colored dolphins painted on the side of the boat that were just above the water line. The dolphins where painted so it gave the appearance that they were leaping from the water. "If that is the same boat, the reason why we can see the dolphins now is because it is lighter. It has just unloaded something very heavy that was keeping it low in the water and hiding the dolphins."

"So it was dropping off something, not picking up a bottle of wine," Cameron said.

"Exactly," Jason said.

Cameron took off her shoes and pocked them down the front of her dress. She lifted her dress where it split up the side and tied it high to her waist.

"What are you doing? I can see your panties," Connor said. "Not that I was looking."

"Connor you're a pervert," Cameron said.

Connor nodded. "Well I'm fourteen and, last time I looked, male. So what's your point?"

"Ugh. Boys are so disgusting. Keep an eye out, I'm going to see what it just unloaded," she said, cocking her leg over the brass rail.

"Why do you hate me?" Connor asked.

"I don't hate you Connor." She smiled. "I just wish you didn't exist."

"Dexter said we are to report back, nothing else," Connor said.

"We can close this mission quick if I can see what they unloaded. And then we can go back to the Infinity campus, and I won't have to share a bathroom with you two gross boys again," Cameron said. She looked at Jason and waited for his reaction. Despite his younger years, she valued his experienced opinion.

"Be careful. Just take a peek and come back. We will keep watch," Jason said, trying to divert his eyes away from her underwear.

She paused and looked at Connor who was still staring at her with her skirt around her waist so she could climb. "Connor, I bet your birth certificate is really just an apology letter from the condom company."

Jason grabbed Connor's arm and pulled him back. "Don't stare at her. Your mind is just like your underwear—dirty, stained, and stinky."

Cameron was a fantastic climber. She had grown up in Alberta, Canada and often climbed the Canadian Rockies with her father. Her slim body with long legs and arms gave her an advantage for climbing or descending a sheer rock face.

It took her no longer than ten minutes to climb down the cliff. She gently lowered herself onto the small jetty that was cut out of the rock face. She let her dress back down and crept along the jetty. She glanced up and could just see Connor and Jason up on the balcony looking down at her. Once she walked passed the speedboat further and deeper along the jetty, they lost sight of her.

She noticed a guard gently moving heavy

crates from the dockside. These were just delivered by the boat with the dolphins painted on the side. Gently, he placed one a time on a trolley and wheeled the crate inside the cavern. He stacked it and came to get another. When he was picking up another to take in, Cameron made her move into the cavern.

It was colder and darker as she got deeper into the cave. Her bare feet made no sound as she crept along the damp stone surface. She noticed an illuminated area ahead and could hear voices. A large room was built into the cave. A guard smoking a cigarette sat in a chair. Across his lap was a semi-automatic rifle.

To avoid the guard, she climbed up into a large cavity in the rock face and discovered an opening. A whole underground warehouse the size of a movie theater was revealed and in the corner sat an office. What she saw next stunned her for a few moments. She had to stop to take it all in. Crate after crate stacked forty foot high. Many had Russian writing on them. She didn't need language skills to read AK-47. The Russian automatic rifle was what filled over four hundred crates.

She climbed into the opening and crept up to another pile of crates. One was open. She checked inside and found it was packed full of Russian RDG5 hand grenades. Another huge stack of crates contained Kalashnikov grenade launchers. More crates contain land mines, Gelignite, and anti-tank rocket launchers.

Cameron tiptoed to the office. She peered inside and was relieved when it was empty. It contained file cabinets and maps on the walls. She spotted a telephone in the corner. Gently, she opened the door, praying it would not squeak, and crept inside. Using the phone, Cameron called Dexter. After four rings it was picked up.

Cameron gave Dexter all the details of everything she had seen. It was more than Dexter needed to raid the castle. He told Cameron to meet up with Connor and Jason, make up an excuse, and leave immediately. Dexter made a call to Infinity, who contacted Turkish Special forces and the Turkish National Police. They were dispatched to the castle immediately. Dexter himself would also go and arrest Weinstein. He would be handed over to the CIA and interrogated.

She put the phone down and crept out of the office. A guard noticed her and shouted. She sprinted towards the jetty, only to come face to face with another guard. He made a grab for her. Cameron lashed out with her foot. Her karate crescent kick to his abdomen took the wind out of him.

Another guard ran towards her and tried to hit her. She twisted his wrist back and kneed him in the groin. Another guard appeared from the stairway. He caught her from behind. Cameron threw her head back, breaking his nose. She followed up, kicking his shin with the heel of her foot. He let her go and cursed at her in Turkish. This gave her the chance to throw a punch into his already broken nose. He yelled in pain and fell to his knees. Cameron ran out towards the jetty and straight into two more guards and Weinstein.

"Cameron, what are you doing here?" Weinstein barked, looking at the three guards she had taken down trying to get to their feet.

"Looking for the ladies room," she said meekly, pausing and looking in all directions before coming to the realization that she was surrounded.

"She was using the phone sir, and she opened a box of grenades," the guard who first saw her said. He caught hold of her arm tightly.

Weinstein looked her up and down and nodded. "It seems I have been foolish. You weren't taking pictures of Bodrum, you were taking them of me. And now your two brothers become friends of my son and daughter. I'm either paranoid or it's a coincidence, and where some people see coincidence, I see conspiracy."

"I was just exploring the castle," Cameron said nervously.

Weinstein looked long and hard at her. "Take her out and feed the sharks," he said to the guard holding her arm. "Your fighting skills are not of a normal sixteen-year-old girl." He looked at one of the guards. "Go and get her brothers. Bring them to me."

"So I know karate, is that a crime? Let me go. You can't hold me," Cameron said, struggling. "My brothers have nothing to do with this."

Another guard approached and drew his sword. He held it to her throat. He gestured her to walk out to the speedboat tied to the jetty. She raised her arms and submitted.

"Looks like you and Ela are getting on well," Jason said to Connor.

"Why of course. She can't resist my charm, good looks, and big biceps," Cameron said, flexing his right arm.

Jason looked back down at the jetty. To his horror, he noticed a guard was holding Cameron and another held a sword to her throat.

They were leading her towards the speedboat.

"They've caught Mosquito Bites," Jason said.

Connor rushed to the side and looked down. "That useless skinny strip of twenty-four-carat ignorance has got herself caught." He cursed.

"You boys need to come with us. Mr. Weinstein wants to talk to you," a guard ordered in broken English. He had another seven guards with him, swarming onto the sun deck.

Jason and Connor looked at each other. "What are you doing to Cameron?" Jason asked.

"Come with us and you won't get hurt," the guard said. He purposely danced his fingers on the handle of his sword that was sheathed on his belt.

Jason looked down at Cameron. They had led her onto the speedboat and started to tie her hands behind her back. A guard attempted to grab for Connor's arm. Connor caught it and twisted it and threw the man across the sundeck. Jason lifted himself onto his toes and stood in a fighting stance.

The guards drew their swords. The razor sharp blades glistened in the sun.

"I'm going to help her. Will you be okay?" Jason asked Connor.

"Sure. I'll meet you down there," Connor said.

Three guards moved forward. Jason ran, ducked, and slid under them towards the table. Connor pounced forward and ducked as a guard swung his sword. Connor picked the guard up and sprinted forward, using the guard as a shield from the others. Several were knocked out of his way as he ploughed through them, his powerful legs pushing forward.

More guards ran towards Connor and Jason. Connor was gaining momentum and speed. The guard he carried was working as a human shield. Connor threw himself and his passenger at the long table. The huge strawberry and bowls of strawberries were thrown into the air. Some of the guests screamed as the table and strawberries came crushing down covering Connor, most of the guards, and some of the guests in soft red sticky strawberry flesh.

Three guards blocked Jason's exit off the sundeck. A foolish guard stepped forward and tried to grab hold of the boy. Jason caught the man's arm and twisted his wrist. He followed with a punch to the man's stomach. The blow was enough to wind the guard. Jason followed up with a powerful roundhouse kick. The force sent the man back several feet into the other two guards, knocking them off their feet.

Jason made his way to the table. He pulled out the parasol that was used for shade and sprinted to the wall. Without a second thought Jason, leapt onto the wall, stepped over the brass rail, and jumped off the side of the sundeck. He held tightly to the parasol, hoping it would act as a parachute and slow his decent. It worked, not as slow as he would have liked, but enough so he wouldn't get hurt. Cameron was tied up and thrown into the speedboat. She and her captors looked up in disbelief as they watched Jason sailing down from the sundeck, hanging from the Parasol.

Jason plunged into the sea. He swam towards the jetty and started to climb out.

"I'll deal with him," Weinstein said, pacing towards Jason. "Well if it's not Mary Poppins. Nice of you to drop in, Jason. You seem to enjoy jumping off rocks into the sea. You can take a trip with your sister to feed the sharks."

Jason stood and pushed his wet, long blond bangs away from his eyes. He forced adrenaline into his system. He knew he was going to need every advantage he had if he was going to take on Weinstein and his guards.

Weinstein charged him with a roar and pace of a raging bull. Jason sidestepped and whirled to face him. His attacker lunged. Jason avoided one flying fist and caught the other, twisting as he held it. Using Weinstein's momentum, Jason threw him across the jetty.

A guard paced towards the boy. Jason noticed him in the corner of his eye and pulled his head back just in time to avoid the blow that was meant for his jaw. Jason could see a blur of knuckles. The guard was fast he attacked again. Jason ducked this time and felt his hair ruffle with the force of it.

Jason dropped to the floor, rolled clear, and sprang up to his feet. Weinstein had recovered. He came from Jason's left side. The guard came again from his right. Jason was surprised. The guard moved fast, so fast that Jason nearly missed seeing it. Jason's body seemed to react on its own, without conscious thought. He slid to his right, opposite to the direction he had been circling, as the guard rushed him. Jason's vision blurred as the battle resumed.

The guard threw a block with his left hand, tried to hook Jason's left leg with his own, trying to throw him to the ground. Jason turned forward and to his right, smashing his left fist against the middle of his opponent's back as he slid past. The blow caught his opponent between his shoulder blades. Jason brought his foot up and caught the guard from behind between the legs. The guard gave a high pitched yelp like a puppy before falling to his knees holding his groin.

Jason had no time to recover. Weinstein grabbed his hair and pulled him back with one hand and punched Jason in the face with the other. Jason spat out blood and cursed at Weinstein. He stepped outside himself, and an anger that should never see the light of day had broken free. Jason pupils fully dilated. He instinctively took several deep breaths, saturating his blood supply with oxygen. His reaction was extreme. Jason threw a vicious punch into Weinstein's windpipe. His knuckles buried themselves deep into Weinstein's throat, crushing his trachea.

As soon as he delivered the near fatal blow, Jason knew he caused serious damage. Weinstein collapsed, holding his throat. He squirmed on the ground, trying to catch a breath. Jason leapt onto the speedboat with a single stride. He threw a side kick at the guard holding Cameron, sending him into the sea.

Jason paused and looked at Cameron. It took him a few seconds to take in his surroundings and calm down.

"Are you just going to stand there or are you going to untie me?" Cameron tutted.

Another guard raced towards him along the jetty with his sword raised. Jason leapt back onto the jetty and ran towards him, As he got close he fell to hip with legs forward and slid towards him, taking out one guard's legs from under him. As the guard fell, Jason caught the handle of his sword and twisted it. The guard had a choice, either have his wrist broken or release his grip on the sword.

Once he had let go of the sword, Jason caught it and threw it into the sea. Jason held the guard down with his arm behind his back. Jason's right hand fumbled for the guard's neck. His fingers found the man's carotid artery and squeezed. The blood supply was blocked, and within a few seconds, the man was unconscious.

Jason ran back to the speedboat and untied Cameron.

"I called Dexter. He's on his way," Cameron said. "Where's Connor?"

"He was on his way here. I'll go and check," Jason panted.

He ran back up the jetty and made his way to the stairs that climbed up to the castle. He climbed a few steps and stopped in his tracks. Connor was walking down the steps. His face was cut, and his nose bleeding. His hands were raised above his head.

Right behind him were two guards both carrying pistols.

"Sorry Jason, I got overpowered," Connor said glumly.

"You boy, hands above your head," one of Connors captors shouted at Jason in broken English.

"You have two chances of that happening, slim and none. And slim just left town," Jason said turning and running back down the stairs. Jason ran towards the office. Two shots rang out, narrowly missing him. Jason ducked behind a stack of crates and peeked out, trying to figure out what to do next.

Connor was forced onto the ground and told not to move. One guard stood over him with a gun pointed at his head. The second guard slowly crept towards the stacks of wooden crates.

Jason looked around for a new hiding place. He found a stack of drums full of fuel, and using all his strength, he tipped one up and rolled it towards the guards.

The guard stopped it rolling with his foot and laughed with his foot resting on the top. He stopped laughing when the cap came off and gas gushed out, making a carpet of deadly flammable gas that started to cover the floor of the cavern.

Jason came out from his place of hiding with a grenade in his right hand and the pin in his left. He was holding the spring trigger tight. If he released his grip, it would explode after a few seconds.

The guard's face turned white. He looked back at the other guard. Both looked terrified and unsure what to do.

"You both need to leave now. If I drop this we all go *bang*," Jason said stating the word 'bang' really loud for good effect. It made both guards jump.

Connor stood. "He's right. He's crazy. You had better go," he said.

"You wouldn't dare," the guard said.

"You have a gun pointed at me, I have nothing else to lose. If I put the grenade down, I'm shark food. If I let it go, we all go *bang*," Jason said again making the bang sound loud and making the guard jump. "So, do you think it wise to dare someone who has nothing else to lose?"

"Come on, I have a family. This kid is loco," the guard said to the other. They both slowly backed away and made their way up the stairway cut out of the rocks. It led up to the castle.

"There are more of his guards upstairs. They may come down," Connor said.

"Get out onto the jetty with Cameron. I will hold them back," Jason said.

"They are armed," Connor suggested.

"I have an idea, go," Jason ordered.

Connor sprinted along the jetty. Cameron was checking Weinstein for a pulse. For a few seconds, Connor watched her, waiting for her diagnoses.

"He's alive but having trouble breathing," Cameron said.

"How did he get like that?" Connor asked.

"Jason hit him," she said softly.

Connor looked at her in disbelief. "Just *hit* him?"

Jason checked the stairway to ensure it was clear. He studied the structure. The stairs where cut out of the rock. They tunneled their way up to the castle. He found a small crevice and dropped the grenade in. Immediately, he jumped down the few stairs and sprinted out towards the jetty.

"Start the boat," Jason shouted as he ran. Cameron looked at the controls.

The grenade exploded, sending shards of rock across the stairway. His plan had failed it didn't block the tunnel as he had hoped. Far worse, some of the gas that had spilled from the gas drum caught fire and started to spread.

"What did you do?" Cameron asked.

"Blocked the tunnel. Let's get out of here," Jason said.

Connor lifted Weinstein and dragged him towards the speedboat. They pulled his unconscious body and let him fall on the deck.

"That's strange," Jason said, looking back at the cavern.

"What is?" Connor asked.

"Where is that smoke coming from and look flames? I only blew up the tunnel entrance," Jason said.

"Derrrrr. Maybe the gas that was everywhere from the huge drum you rolled across the floor," Connor said.

Flames started to come out of the cavern. Smoke billowed its way up to the castle. The guests panicked and left out onto the street at the back of the castle.

"I think we better go. That place is full of grenades and all sorts of weaponry. It's gonna go Ka Boom!" Cameron said. She started the speedboat. Jason untied it from its moorings.

Seconds after the motor started to churn the water and propel the speedboat away, an explosion was heard followed, by another and another. Then, the whole lot blew. An ear-shattering explosion cracked the air as if the belly of hell itself had opened up. The blast of hot air lifted Connor from his feet and threw him onto his back on the deck next to Weinstein. He blinked up into the smoke covered sky; raindrops glowed orange as they fell towards the earth.

Rocks splintered into the sea, coming at the speedboat like mortar shells. Slowly, a large part of the castle collapsed into itself. The sea facing wall and sun deck where they had all previous stood fell and was swallowed whole by the sea. Another explosion and the castle completely fell into itself. The explosion could be heard thirty miles away. The entire town shook.

By the time the smoke had cleared, the castle, some surrounding buildings, and half the rock face had disappeared into the depths of the sea.

Connor and Cameron look wide-eyed at the carnage. Cameron slowed the speedboat down to a crawl. She and Connor looked at Jason.

"Oops," Jason said meekly. Nothing else seemed appropriate.

"*Oops*?" Connor shouted. "You blew up half the town."

"I've only been at Infinity a couple of months. I got graded 'C' in explosives. I can see why now," Jason said.

CHAPTER TWENTY THREE

Dexter and his three fictitious children were to spend one final night in Bodrum before returning back to Infinity. Jason said nothing about the fight he had with Weinstein. Cameron told Dexter that Jason had saved her, he fought two guards and Weinstein. No one argued or aforementioned that Jason had used too much force. Three adults against one thirteen-year-old were bad odds.

Dexter called Jason into his room for a debrief. Jason's face had a cut over his eye, and it had swollen and was turning into a dark bruise.

"Jason, you guys all did a great job. However, Cameron should never have climbed down the rock face. She could have been killed. And you can't fly off buildings using a parasol. We don't need to take risks like that. That said, the case is now closed. We have enough to put Weinstein away for years, that is, if he recovers. The doctors had to operate on his throat. You almost killed him," Dexter said in a way that sounded like a reprimand to Jason.

"Oh, so him punching me in the face and taking Cameron out to sea to chop up and use as a shark snack is okay as long as I don't hurt him?" Jason said.

Dexter studied Jason and nodded. "As for the nine hundred old castle, it was a famous landmark that is gone forever. Are you able to control your temper?"

"I was high on adrenaline. He punched me. Hard. And if the castle was that old, maybe it's time they built a new one," Jason said.

"Jason, you're a skilled martial artist. You know how not to hit someone or how to kill someone. What was going through your mind when you hit Weinstein?" Dexter asked.

"I had lost my temper sir. I can't control it if I get hurt or see someone I care about. I explode. No pun intended. When I was in Northern Ireland and this guy punched Scott... I went berserk and did some serious damage to the guy, and almost hurt Scott after. I was so angry I just couldn't stop. The adrenaline I can pull into my system is a great defense mechanism. Only a few karate grand masters in China can perform it. My teacher Wong Tong taught me because I was so small against older boys. I have developed it and can turn it on at will." Jason paused and smiled. "I just can't find the off switch."

"I see, and it's worse when you lose your temper?" Dexter asked, showing genuine concern.

Jason gave a tight-lipped smile and sucked on his top lip. "In Vietnam, there was a naval officer called Cookie. I really liked him; he made me laugh. He was injured, and then this general shot and killed him in front of me. I hit him with a deadly blow and used everything in my power and knowledge to make the strike a lethal as it could be. It worked, and I even broke some fingers doing it."

"When I lose my temper I kinda go crazy. Weinstein punched me pretty hard. I may be an expert at martial arts, but I'm still a thirteen-year-old boy. I feel pain like anyone my age. So I lost my temper," Jason said.

"You did well Jason. Without you, Cameron could have been killed and maybe thousands of more people would be getting killed or injured by the weapons you destroyed. George Young wrote in your file you go too far sometimes but said it was worth it," Dexter said before Jason interrupted him.

"I liked George Young. I'm going to miss him," Jason said sadly.

"I agree with George. You may have a few issues with a temper, but overall, you are worth it. My report to Infinity will be positive. We would not have done it without you. However, you should have thought before you tried to block the stairwell by blowing up part of the wall. Luckily, the smoke raised the alarm and everyone fled. We don't think any innocent people died. Although, when the cavern collapsed, two guards were crushed."

"Yeah, I would have been disappointed too." Jason grinned. His grin was soon wiped off his face when he noticed Dexter's face change and disapproval of his joke.

Jason looked at Dexter. "I'm sorry. I never meant to blow the whole place up." Jason paused. "When I get back to Infinity, I'm going to find a Sayokan karate school in Istanbul."

Dexter sighed. "We don't normally have students leave Infinity for additional training. I will have to ask and see if it's possible. I doubt you will get a pass Jason, and currently, I would advise you to keep your head down."

"It's not up for debate. I'm doing it. I have mastered three styles and Judo and want to learn many more. I'm living in Turkey. It makes perfect sense to practice Sayokan," Jason said.

"And I take it if we refuse you what, leave Infinity? Come, Jason why do you need more? You have three black belts. You are third Dan in one. Plus, you have black belt in Judo. Can't you be content with that?" Dexter pleaded.

"Someone who is content has lost all ambition, and someone without ambition is already dead. Wong Tong said that, and I agree with him. Today, I came across a good fighter, someone with good martial art skills. If I had stopped at one black belt, maybe he would have beaten me. Cameron and I would both be dead. If Infinity wants me to work for them, I will but, I'm still learning and improving. Martial arts means more to me than anything else," Jason said. He looked serious and spoke in a manner that surprised Dexter.

"I have never known anyone who likes martial arts as much as you. You treat it like a religion." Dexter paused and folded his arms across his chest and nodded. "I know you're like a hot house plant. You can't grow under natural conditions. You need a purpose, something challenging and strenuous. But I also know you need love and need security to survive. I will make sure you get a pass so you can study Sayokan." Dexter smiled.

"Jason, you are like a grenade, and at some point you are going to go off. I want to minimize the casualties when that happens. So it's safer for everyone to keep you at Infinity, and we have orders to keep you here and keep you safe of course"… Dexter trailed off.

"Orders. Orders from who?" Jason asked.

"Let's just say, someone in a very high place who knows about Infinity insisted you study here. I can't say, but it's for your own good. You are much better suited to being taught at Infinity than any school in London," Dexter said as a matter of fact.

Jason thanked him and kept his thoughts to himself, although, he suspected the orders came from Catherine's mother, the queen.

When he had been in Northern Ireland at the church with the O'Neills, he respected their religion, and he respected Cailin's family's religion. It gave them all a faith to believe in something. Wong Tong told Jason of the Chinese Buddha. At his first school, Jason made friends from around the world, some who followed a Muslim or Jewish faith. It left him confused because adults of the same faith would fight and start wars. Jason chose to follow martial arts. It gave him a sense of wellbeing. It kept him fit, alive, strong, and had saved the lives of others. It was Jason's religion.

After a light breakfast, Jason strolled down to the beach. He needed some time to himself. A time when he could be himself without obligations and a time to reflect on his own thoughts. He sat on a rock watching a boy no more than four or five with his mother playing in sand. It brought back a memory when he was six. His grandparents had flown out to see him in Hong Kong and had taken him to the beach for the first time.

It reminded him almost too vividly of the hot velvet sand and the painful grit of wet sands between his young, tender toes. He wondered what ever happened to the precious pile of seashells he and his grandmother collected. For a few years, they had been on his windowsill. Fond memories of his grandfather showing him to look under seaweed in rock-pools and finding tiny crabs that tried to scurry away. How far he had come from the carrot cake and ice cream suppers with lemonade mixed with a splash of his grandfather's beer.

His pleasant thoughts were rudely disturbed when he was smacked in the side of the face by a large ball of wet, sandy seaweed. Before he could remove the clingy cold wet green slime and see where it came from, he could heard Connor bursting with laughter.

Jason screamed a curse and chased him. Connor sprinted up through the town with Jason in hot pursuit. For over a mile, Connor ran up and down the streets and eventually into the center of Bodrum. Jason was a few feet behind him, almost able to catch him. Connor kept going as fast as he could.

Eventually, Connor slipped and fell. He rolled onto his back, still laughing. "You should have seen your face." Connor roared with laughter, his face red from exhaustion and laughter.

Jason pounced on him, pinning him down on the ground. He cursed again and started to laugh himself. He climbed off Connor and lay on the ground next to him, trying to get his breath back.

"That was so funny Jason. You were really angry." Connor panted. "I laughed so much my stomach is hurting."

"I owe you one now. When you least expect it, I'm gonna get you back." Jason laughed.

For a few moments, they lay in the middle of the street taking in the sun before a car honked, forcing them to climb to their feet. The town was still trying to recover from the large explosion. Local townsfolk were astonished to find out that their beloved town was being used to store and sell arms all over the world. None would ever guess that the two boys playing in the street were responsible for blowing up a part of the town.

Back at Infinity, Connor, Cameron, and Jason were treated like heroes. Jason and Connor stayed close friends. Cameron actually smiled whenever she saw either of them. Although if any of her friends were looking, she would ignore them. Jason started Sayokan karate, and in mid-July, went home for two weeks to see his friends and family.

Jason never found out exactly who had intervened and got him a place at Infinity. All he was told was it someone very high up. The only person who he could think of was also the same person who did not want him seeing her daughter. He wasn't sure if he should be grateful to her for getting him a place at Infinity or angry for her trying to keep him out of London. He concluded he would just put the idea out of his thoughts.

Ray and Brenda picked Jason up at London's Heathrow airport. Jason was given a hug and kiss from his father, followed by the same from Brenda. Jason wasn't sure what he thought of being kissed and hugged by Brenda. He still thought of her as Battle Axe Brenda.

"Did you notice anything different about Brenda?" Ray asked as they walked to the car.

Jason looked her up and down. "Yeah, she's grown four inches." He shrugged.

"No Jason, be serious. Look again," Ray said holding her hand with one hand and carrying Jason case with the other.

"Are you pregnant?" Jason asked.

"Oh my, no Jason." Brenda laughed. She held out her left hand and flashed a shiny diamond ring at him. "Your father proposed to me."

Jason looked at his father and Brenda, unsure what to say at first. "Um. Congratulations. So no baby then?" Jason asked.

"No Jason, we have you, and that's enough for now." Ray smiled.

CHAPTER TWENTY FOUR

The black pants and sweater with the infinity logo was gone, and Jason was somewhat more comfortable in his jeans and T-shirt. For two weeks, he was home, and it felt good to be in his own room. Jason found it strange having Brenda in the house. He could no longer walk in the kitchen in just his underwear. Jason adapted and went along with the changes, because he noticed how happy his father was.

Scott arrived the following day. He was going to stay for a few days. Jason struggled to keep Infinity a secret. He tried to change the subject every time Scott asked about his school until Scott found his school report.

"German, A plus. French, A plus. Spanish, A plus. Japanese, A minus. Who's a nerd now?" Scott teased before continuing.

"Martial Arts, A plus. Rural Studies, B plus, and aim is improving. English, A Minus. Jase, your grades are awesome. You must like this school." Scott asked.

"I do, it's great. Put it down, we are on school break now," Jason said taking his report back. "Shall we go into town and see what movie is on?"

"Rural Studies. What's that?" Scott asked.

"Oh, that's em, you know farming stuff, about wheat and animals. Shall we go to the movies then?" Jason said, trying to change the subject.

Scott looked at Jason. "What do they mean your aim is improving?"

Jason colored up. He thought about saying aim for higher grades but didn't like the idea of lying to his best friend, so he said nothing.

After a minute's silence, Scott approached Jason and looked at him directly in the eyes. "Jason, you know I can work out a puzzle and have double your IQ. Don't lie to me."

"I didn't lie to you. I would never lie to you. We are best friends. That would be like lying to myself," Jason objected.

"Then answer my question. What is Rural Studies?"

Jason sighed and sat down heavily on his bed with his head down. "I can't say." Although as soon as he said it, he knew it would just provoke Scott to ask more questions.

"It's not a normal school, is it?" Scott suggested.

"You've gotta promise you won't say anything. Even my dad doesn't know or Brenda," Jason said.

Scott sat down next to Jason. "Do you really have to ask that of me?"

Jason told Scott everything regarding Infinity. He felt better for telling someone. Scott looked stunned by the information but believed it, and it was obvious that Jason was happy at Infinity.

"So does this mean we won't both be working together for MI6?" Scott said. "Maybe I can work for Infinity?"

"Um, they already looked at you and… Well, they said you didn't have the full package, meaning you would be no good out on a mission," Jason said. "Although, I tried sticking up for you."

"Thanks, but I'm allergic to pain, sports, danger, fighting, shooting, and anything other than a nice warm office." Scott laughed.

"I like it at Infinity. I feel at home, and being in Turkey has its advantages. It's warm, sunny, and I get to learn a new form of martial arts," Jason said.

The two weeks flew by. Jason managed to spend an afternoon with Princess Catherine at Buckingham Palace before going back to Istanbul and rejoining Infinity. They bumped into her mother in a hallway. After the pleasantries and hellos, she told Jason she was proud of what he was doing in Turkey. Jason realized it must have been the Queen who Quinton Roosevelt was referring too when he mentioned that Jason had been recommended to Infinity by someone at the highest level.

He wondered what his new life would bring. How many more people would he get close to before having to say goodbye for good?

William Weinstein spent the rest of his life in prison. Ela and Farah were put into a foster home. Was the world a better place without Weinstein dealing arms to terrorists? Jason had to hope it was.

*

Within a few weeks, an elderly man sat at a café in Amsterdam sipping Earl Grey tea. He looked unlike any tourist. He was impeccably dressed in a Savile Row suit. He sipped his tea and twiddled with his handlebar moustache. His foot tapped gently in beat with the piano accordionist who serenaded diners. A thirty-four foot yacht launch pulled up to the riverbank.

Two men jumped ashore and fastened it to the jetty before checking up and down the busy promenade. The elderly man gently placed his cup in the saucer and marched towards his car that was parked just a few feet from the yacht. He stood by the trunk and waited. A bald headed man wearing a white suit stepped off the yacht, closely followed by two bodyguards. He looked the elderly man up and down. He smiled, although his face was badly scarred caused by an explosion many years ago, so you couldn't tell if he was smiling or about to burst out in tears.

He passed a briefcase of cash to the elderly gentleman who responded by opening his trunk. The two bodyguards picked up four large wooden crates full of AK-47 Russian assault rifles. They carried them back to the motor yacht.

"So it seems you are the new guy to go to now Weinstein has become careless?" the bald man said in a deep Russian accent. "You can check the money if you want. It's all there. What do I call you?"

"You don't. If you need something, go via the underground route with your order. They will get it to me," the gentleman scoffed in his upper crust British accent.

"But what do I call you?" The bald man asked, lighting a large Cuban cigar and blowing a large smoke ring into the air.

"SS."

The elderly man who called himself SS climbed into his black Mercedes and drove off with his case of cash.

The secret underground world of arms deals that brought misery to thousands of lives had a new player. A man with no name other than SS, no family, no home. But most dangerous of all, he was a man who thought he was untouchable to the world's most successful secret agent. Was he tempting fate? Did he know that one day his time would come? Would he ever come face to face with Jason Steed again? And if he did, what would be the outcome?

For now, Jason would continue at Infinity. Unbeknownst to him, it was for own safety. The criminal underworld had been made to look foolish yet again at the hands of a boy. Many in the Triad had not forgiven how he and George Young had almost destroyed the British network. Now, some of the worst terrorist groups, including the IRA, been weakened and belittled by the same boy.

In his favor, he had saved many lives and prevented much misery, death, and the pain of thousands. For this, his friends in high places would cast a net of protection over him with a decree to shelter him from harm. Despite the Royal Decree, SYUI, Infinity, and his family and friends, Jason was often very much alone. And when it came down to his safety, he could only ever rely on one person in the world to protect him and who he could trust fully. That person was called Jason Steed.

The Jason Steed series
by Mark A. Cooper.

Book 1 **FLEDGLING JASON STEED**

Book 2 **REVENGE JASON STEED**

Book 3 **JASON STEED ABSOULTELY NOTHING**

Book 4 **JASON STEED BY ROYAL DECREE**

Other books by this author

EDELWEISS PIRATES 'Operation Einstein'

CPSIA information can be obtained at www.ICGtesting.com
Printed in the USA
LVOW08s2021300315

432596LV00020B/241/P